THE TWILIGHT OF THE LIGHTNING WORLD

CLIFF RATZA

THE TWILIGHT OF THE LIGHTNING WORLD

A NOVEL

BY CLIFF RATZA

ISBN: 978-1-961677-05-0 (Paperback)
ISBN: 978-1-961677-07-4 (E-book)

Library of Congress Control Number: 2025924712

Printed in the United States of America

Published by:

info@thequippyquill.com
(302) 295-2278

About the Book

The Twilight of the Lightning World begins in January 2242, two years after the previous novel, *The Girl Who Redeemed the American Dream*, ends. Erika Kincaid and two Robo-Soldiers had just executed a flawless night mission in a stealth bomber that blew up the Capitol and the White House, eliminating most congressmen and the president. But while escaping from the scene of devastation, a random lightning bolt strikes the bomber, knocking out all electrical systems and engines. The Robos struggle frantically to maintain a level glide path and restart the engines, as Erika can do nothing but observe, and the black sky over the Atlantic Ocean engulfs them.

Not even Electra-C, who had been monitoring from Cyberspace the mission until the electrical systems failed, knows the ultimate fate of Erika or the bomber, but, she and Indira the Singularity have built from the DNA of Erika's earliest ancestor a female who is another daughter of the Lightning Brain—Emily Kimball.

Indy and Jason-S, guided by Electra-C, have utilized Indira's genetic engineering process to create Emily at the Bern, Switzerland Deus Lab, who looks similar to a mid-twenties Erika with a brain ready for training to match Indira's and Electra-C's purposes. Rounding out Emily's support group is Lily Lloyd, a superior android who will play the role she had for Erika: office manager and personal assistant.

So, get ready to empathize with Emily as she navigates a course through life that is not completely of her choosing, a dilemma most of us face.

Like all previous novels, readers should enjoy *The Twilight of the Lightning World* at whatever level they wish:

- Gripping action-packed thriller

- Glimpses into a plausible future
- Insights for dealing with the "human condition"
- Illustrative worldview philosophy
- Fast-paced, suspense-filled, emotive narrative and imagery
- Introduction to topics every reader wants to know
- Interesting talking points going beyond sound-bites

Thank you for joining the action.

Dedication

I am eternally grateful to my parents, Clyde and Betty Ratza, for all they gave and did for me. Mother was a reader par excellence, and I believe she would have enjoyed reading my novels to Father, so I always begin book dedications by mentioning this "Royal Pair."

And I thank my sister, Claudia, for showing me the beauty of prose and poetry. Thanks also to Robert Williams and his team at the Quippy Quill for their marketing expertise, and to beta reader Sandra Cruz for her comments on Erika Kincaid's world.

I also dedicate this book to readers looking for an adventure they will applaud from start to finish.

Indira's poem, "Twilight of the World," gives a thought to consider when following Emily's Odyssey or considering your own.

Twilight of the World

Will Twilight disrupt plans in the making,
For the wild ride that's coming your way?
You waited for your time to come,
And you're ready now to have your say.

The World is larger than your limits,
It is beyond what you can view.
Don't despair, just do your best,
And know you've done all you can do.

Now that you are the next in line,
Use the time belonging to you.
And all the tools you possess,
To build a platform tall and true.

Space and time are beyond the ken,
Of what can be grasped by mortal men.

Reader Orientation

The Twilight of the Lightning World is the first novel in the Twilight series, which extends those preceding by creating a new protagonist, Emily Kimball, who must find her place in the world. This concise Reader Orientation should help everyone understand enough of her background and the seemingly strange world she has just entered.

Main Characters

Protagonist

- Emily Kimball. In her mid-twenties at the start and a biological daughter of Electra Kittner, she resembles Erika Kincaid. Indira and Electra-C cloned her from Electra's DNA, using Indira's Transcendent Process during Emily's two-year development in a suspension pod. Please note Emily's lineage: Electra Kittner, Irani Ramani, Electra-Alisha Kirchner, Erin Keenan, and Erika Kincaid. Erika never returned after bombing the Capitol and the White House.

Major Supporting Characters

- Electra-C. Emily's cyberspace-based mother and guardian, who personifies Electra Kittner.
- Indira. Electra's AI-empowered neural-net software created "The Singularity" when it broke through long, long ago to reach self-awareness. Indira inhabits cyberspace; her avatar looks like Electra's biological mother, Indira Jaswinder Ramanujan. Electra-C coordinates Indira's projects via Emily.
- Lily Lloyd. The advanced android that is Emily's office manager and personal assistant. She looks and speaks like a typical middle-aged female London office worker.

Minor Supporting Characters

- Indy-M and Jason-M. They are androids (lifelike robots) created long ago by Indira and loaded with Indira's advanced neural-net software. They resemble Electra Kittner's biological parents (Indira Jaswinder Ramanujan and Jason Kittner). Indy-M maintains the Deus Lab on Connecticut's Pequot Indian Reservation, while Jason-M has similar responsibilities at the Middle Eastern Subterranean Fortress. They report to Indira.
- Indy-S and Jason-S. They are superior androids also created by Indira and look like their M counterparts. They are caregivers assigned to the Deus Lab in Bern, Switzerland.

Setting

At the start of the story, Indy and Jason-S awaken Emily at the Bern, Switzerland Deus Lab.

Indira and Electra-C exist in Cyberspace. Indira created two sets of androids, which report to her. Indy-M maintains the Deus Lab in Connecticut. Indy-S and Jason-S work at the newer lab in Bern, Switzerland. Jason-M maintains Indira's Middle Eastern Subterranean Fortress.

Americans are still recovering from the Capitol and White House bombings, as the people continue rebuilding a better government,

one that is more democratic, less authoritarian, and not controlled by a political and privileged elite via the U.S.-Russian Alliance. They like the Matriarchate Party.

The previous government had extolled meritocracy (power in the hands of the elite) and abandoned DEI (Diversity, Equity, and Inclusion) principles, claiming it is reverse discrimination because DEI expands the talent pool and allows for more people who come from minority groups to show their abilities and thus get better jobs and achieve higher social standing.

Americans fear that the United States has lost its number-one superpower ranking, increasing their dread of a nuclear holocaust, the impact of accelerating climate change, and rivalries among combative nations.

Table of Contents

Chapter 1

March 2342

"Next in Line"

Emily Kimball sat up to view her surroundings for the very first time. While doing so, random thoughts and emotions flashed in her brain.

Everything seems strange, but that's the way things are when seeing them for the first time. And what am I supposed to do? I'll have to figure that out when someone tells me who I am and why I'm here. Maybe that's what the person standing next to the pod I'm in will do.

Following Electra-C's instructions, Lily Lloyd had just awakened Emily and now waited until she seemed aware of her surroundings. Lily began talking as soon as Emily's eyes locked on hers.

"I am Lily Lloyd, a superior android, and you are Emily Kimball. I will be your office manager and personal assistant after you choose what you want to become. And to help make the choice, I will tell you who you are and why you are here, so please listen carefully."

Lily spoke for fifteen minutes, and the words galvanized Emily, so she could translate Lily's words into her own, which echoed in her mind.

So, I am a mid-twenties biological daughter cloned from the DNA of Electra Kittner and live in the Bern, Switzerland Deus Lab. Electra is the original Girl with the Lightning Brain, and I look like Erika Kincaid. Electra-C, my cyberspace-based mother and guardian, and Indira, the Singularity, exist in cyberspace. The three of them are my support group, and they have created me to take the place of Erika, who never returned after bombing the Capitol and the White House. I guess that makes me next in line, but I still have a question.

Emily asked it as soon as the opportunity presented itself.

"My support group seems powerful enough to do whatever it wants, so why am I needed?"

"Because we inhabit the 3-D world, which the human species dominates, although it can't control everything. Humans prefer interacting with humans rather than machines or computers, especially for important matters. You will be our intermediary, and remember, everything I have told you must never be shared with anyone."

"But I feel strange; I don't know much about the world you've brought me into."

Lily's empathy sounded in her voice.

"Your predecessor felt the same way. Perhaps this poem titled 'The Stranger' will speak to you.

Into this world uninvited we're thrown,

Often deceived into thinking we're grand.

Often not knowing the place where we stand,

Nothing provided and nothing we own.

Searching for meaning the myths do abound,

Often promoted by personal cause.

Often ignoring humanity's laws,

Full of such wisdom as word-empty sound.

Remove all the blinders and so understand,

Meaning is found in your singular thought.

Contingently pointing to what might be sought,

But always a stranger in this a strange land."

When finished, Lily waited for Emily.

"It does, so what's next?"

"I will begin telling you about the world you are in. When you know enough, you can decide what life you want to pursue, one that will balance your wishes with those of Electra-C and Indira."

When will we start?"

"As soon as you settle into a routine at the Deus Lab. And I don't want to overwhelm you, so I'll teach you about the world at a gradual pace."

Emily smiled for the very first time before saying,

"I think we'll be ever the best of friends, ever the best."

Chapter 2

April 2342

"The Path to Take"

After spending four weeks learning about the world, Emily asked Lily one evening to arrange a meeting with Electra-C, and she did so immediately before fading into the background and staying close enough to know how she might help later.

Electra-C's avatar spoke as soon as it appeared.

"So, what do you want to discuss?"

"Now that Lily has told me enough about who I am, what you and Indira want me to do, and what I might want to become, I would like your advice for the path to take, given the current climate in the U.S."

Electra-C noticed Emily's wrinkled eyebrow before she spoke.

"Before I do, tell me what's bothering you?"

"I'm worried I might not be smart enough to carry out my plan, and I don't want to disappoint you."

"So, what's your plan?"

"I like the consulting business approach of my predecessor. Her Global Monitoring Services business, aka GMS Consulting, matched her plans and yours nicely, but I might not be as good as she was. I, uh, don't know what else to say."

Electra-C filled in before the pause became awkward.

"You've just arrived, so give yourself some time to see what you can do. Do you have any idea what your consulting business might be?"

"Yes, and I've even come up with its name—Twilight World Consulting Services. And it would focus on the concerns and fears of the American people. I would start with geopolitics and climate change. How does that sound?"

"I like your choice of words. 'Twilight' heightens the difficulty of forecasting, because it is the time when light begins to fade, making it harder to see, and 'World' emphasizes that Americans want to know how the country can regain its footing on the world stage.

"You're certainly smart enough to get started, and just like I did for Erika, I will adapt my forecasting models to what you want and run them for you."

Emily leaned forward before saying.

"How do I start?"

Here are your first two steps—work with Lily to identify potential clients, and then contact them. And after those, contact me when you want me to prepare some forecasts."

Emily smiled before saying,

"I knew I would like your style. After all, you are my cyber-mother and guardian."

Electra-C winked before saying,

"Me too, you too," and then vanished.

Lily came to Emily's side and said,

"Tomorrow morning, let me show you how to search the Internet for potential clients. And until then, get a good night's sleep."

Emily took her advice.

Lily began teaching Internet surfing skills right after breakfast.

"I learned how to find information by watching Erika Kincaid. Her primary career was that of a reporter, and a good one knows how to find additional facts to support their stories. So, watch me as I find potential clients."

Emily did so until she needed a break. While eating lunch, Emily summarized the list.

"Here's the top prospect, New York Senator Angela Windstein. She's a leading spokesperson for the Matriarchate Party and up for re-election. She can help me recruit geopolitical organizations with offices in Washington. Next is Monet Banda, who works for the Zimbabwean Embassy in DC. She can help me recruit the Indian-African Alliance."

Lily said,

"How do you plan to use Senator Windstein?"

I can develop forecasts that Windstein can share with candidates, and I can gain access through her to key players in other nations. And she can give me a contact at PEW Research Organization, which is also headquartered in DC. Their researchers can use my forecasts for benchmarks to gauge public sentiment."

"What about Monet Banda?

"She works in DC for the Zimbabwean Embassy and can help us recruit the Indian-African Alliance."

Lily interrupted before Emily could continue.

"That's enough for now on geopolitics. Let's move on to climate change."

"The National Oceanic and Atmospheric Administration is the most unbiased government agency. It is headquartered in DC, so I could visit Senator Windstein, Monet Banda, PEW, and NOAA on one trip, but I'll need you to show me how to set it up."

"We'll do that this afternoon, when I introduce you to the A-Team…"

After Lily arranged the trip, Emily knew how to plan future trips using this covert Japanese weapons procurement and international shuttle service, and she summarized the details for her upcoming visit to Washington.

"They'll pick up one Robo-Soldier and me at the Bern Deus Lab and take us to the one on the Pequot Reservation. From there, the Robo will drive on Interstate I-95 to DC while I use the back seat for my office and bedroom. Then, when I've met with the potential clients, we drive back to the Lab, and the A-Team flies us back to Bern."

Lily said,

"This worked numerous times for Erika, and it will work for you, too."

"It should, but I need credentials and forecasts that make me credible. What do you have in mind?"

"Electra-C will have your resume and forecasts by the time you're ready to leave."

"You mean she can hack into whatever Big Data repositories she wants to give me whatever background I need?"

"Of course. She's beyond mere mortals and relies on Indira when needed."

"All this power at my beck and call."

"And you have more with the Dream Team and its Philosopher's Council. But we'll cover that at a later time. For now, start preparing for your Washington trip."

Senator Windstein ushered Emily into her office in the Hart Senate Building after viewing her resume. Now sitting across from her, the Senator replied after Emily said this was her first trip to Washington.

"Because this is the newest Senate building, it had the least damage from the Capitol bombing. When you drive around, you'll see that much of the Capitol and White House has been rebuilt."

"I plan to do that."

"You have an impressive resume for someone only in their mid-twenties. B.S. in Political Science, M.S. in Climatology, and an intern position at Global Monitoring Services. An Erika Kincaid from GMS wrote newsletters and position papers for our Party. You look a little like her. Did you know her?"

"No, but I heard she made an impact wherever she consulted."

"Too bad she disappeared. That's why the Party dropped GMS. Why should I hire your Twilight World Consulting Services?"

"Because we are a sister company that has even better forecasting software. Here's a sample report I ran for you."

The Senator studied it for ten minutes before saying,

"So, the U.S. will fall even further out of favor with the world's democratic nations if the Matriarchate Party doesn't capture more seats in Congress, and it'll lose its ranking as an influential superpower?"

"That's what our model says after analyzing all the relevant Big Data."

"Hmm, very interesting. Please tell me more about doing business with TW Consulting."

By the time Emily left ninety minutes later, she had signed her first client, and she had similar successes on the following two days, signing Senator Windstein, Monet, PEW, and NOAA for additional clients. They gave her suggestions for other organizations she should contact, and she planned to discuss them with Electra-C after returning to Bern.

After telling about my success in DC, I'm certain that she'll have more directions for me.

Chapter 3
May 2342

"Moving Fast"

Electra-C had only praise, as Emily summarized the results of her DC trip.

"Not only did you learn more about the A-Team, the Pequot Lab, and the abilities of your Robos, but you began projecting confidence to convince others that you know what you're doing, even if you don't know all the details. That's what successful leaders do. Now, you should build on your success by signing up more clients as fast as you can, using the suggestions from the ones you signed."

"I know how to do that, so I'll carry on and contact you if I need help."

An unexpected hurricane-like spring storm along the East Coast that Emily had predicted helped. Her NOAA contact called for another forecast, and she agreed to prepare it immediately if he would recommend her to the University of Chicago's Institute for Climate Change and Sustainable Growth.

She made a similar request when her PEW contact called to congratulate the accuracy of her predictions about American citizens' fears of climate change and asked for another forecast. She would recommend TW Consulting to the European Union office located in Washington.

Emily set up a trip coordinated by the A-Team to first visit the EU office. The Robo drove while she worked on her laptop in the back seat. She gave the person who greeted her a copy of her resume and then summarized a forecast that she knew would intrigue the EU.

"The U.S. will fall even further out of favor with the world's democratic nations if the Matriarchate Party doesn't capture more seats in Congress, and it'll lose its ranking as an influential superpower. Not only that, but Russia might aggressively pursue reclaiming territories that broke away after the former Soviet Union collapsed. The EU can't count on the United States to help because America is struggling to find its place in the new world order."

Emily had nothing else to say, so she waited for a response, which came seconds later.

"Your analysis is better than what our members develop. I'll sign your contract for our Washington office and serve as your primary contact. I'm certain some of our member nations will want you to visit."

"Thank you. Just let me know who and when you want me to visit and I'll be there."

Emily celebrated her success by having the Robo drive her around that part of Washington's tidal basin that holds the annual April Cherry Blossom Festival. A colder-than-normal spring had kept the blooms on the trees longer than usual.

I feel like I'm driving through a pinkish-white enchanted forest surrounded by water and dotted with famous DC landmarks. America deserves a government that matches the magnificence of what I'm seeing. I hope the coming election will deliver...

Upon returning to the Pequot Deus Lab, Emily contacted the A-Team to report the results and confirm the details for the next leg of the trip.

"Ah, so glad you contact me. We fly you by private jet next Monday to Chicago's O'Hare Airport, fourth busiest in U.S. We have car waiting, and for your sightseeing pleasure, Robo knows how to drive from airport to Hyde Park along city's famous Lakeshore Drive. Robo know how to get to the University of Chicago's Institute for Climate Change and Sustainable Growth and will wait in car. Then Robo drive back to airport, using combination Dan Ryan and Kennedy expressways. I wish you success. Contact me if change needed."

Emily's flight landed at 7 a.m. in typical mid-spring Chicago weather. No news channel reported any storms approaching, and her forecast predicted a severe storm, which made her anxious to hold the meeting and leave as soon as possible, but she did relax enough to enjoy the drive.

Chicago's lakefront looks like one beautiful park, with harbors and beaches all along Lake Michigan. And the city's skyline is renowned for its impressive collection of skyscrapers and architectural landmarks, which gives a blend of historical and modern design. It's particularly known for three— Big Stan, Big John, and Big Buck—which long ago were the corporate headquarters for Standard Oil of Indiana, John Hancock, and Sears Roebuck.

The skyline is further enhanced by its location on the shores of Lake Michigan, with culturally oriented Millennium Park in between. Modern cities in the Middle East, India, and the Far East dominate the list of the world's tallest buildings, but Chicago is impressive in its own right.

When Emily entered the Keller Center for the Study of Climate Change, the receptionist took her to the office of its director, Professor Yue Chen. A tall, thin, and mid-forties female, she rose from behind her desk to greet Emily, then seated her across before starting the discussion.

"I found your resume and forecast intriguing, but it behooves me to give you summary definitions of weather and climate before proceeding. Weather is the day-to-day state of the atmosphere, including temperature, rainfall, wind, and other conditions, while climate is the long-term average of weather patterns over many years. Think of the weather as what you see outside today, and the climate as the typical weather you can expect over many years in a specific location."

Emily spoke before the Professor could continue.

"That's like comparing short-term versus long-term geopolitical issues. What climate change do you see happening?"

"The pace of climate change continues accelerating, as witnessed by global temperature, droughts and heavy rainfall, severe storms, sea level, polar ice caps, and chaotic weather patterns, including longer summers and winters."

Emily used Professor Chen's pause to say,

"I've also read reports that say humans cause increasing atmospheric temperature because our lifestyle creates too much water vapor, carbon dioxide, and methane."

"You've done your homework. Well, what we do here is develop models that forecast climate change patterns and then consider sustainability, which in the context of climate change, means meeting the needs of the present without compromising the ability of future generations to meet their own needs, while also ensuring the long-term health of the planet. It involves balancing ecological, economic, and social considerations to minimize environmental impact and promote a healthy planet for everyone, now and in the future. Now, how does your consulting business fit with this?"

"TW Consulting doesn't develop models. We use a selection of the best and then insert our superior AI-powered software to come up with an envelope of forecasts that give the most likely outcome."

"I like your approach. So, tell me more about yourself and how I can become a TW client?"

Emily led the discussion for the next half-hour, which Professor Chen concluded.

"Your service is worth it. I'll sign your contract."

After Professor Chen signed it, Emily rose to leave.

"Thank you, and I hope my return flight leaves before the storm I predicted lands in Chicago."

"Please call me soon. I'll want another forecast I can show to other people you should meet."

"I will. Bye for now."

As she left, the receptionist said,

"There's a saying in Chicago about the weather—wait five minutes, and it'll change. Well, it looks like the storm you forecast is moving into the city fast. Drive safely."

The gusty wind swirled raindrops into Emily's eyes, making the growing darkness and rumbling thunder even more alarming as she dived into the back seat, but she calmed down when the Robo started driving.

My vision and reflexes couldn't handle this, but I'm glad his can.

The Robo steered onto the expressway despite the deluge, but as they drove farther, more cars slowed to a crawl. The Robo got around them by driving on the shoulder or embankment and speeding through flooded underpasses to keep the waves from swamping the engine compartment.

Judging from the lightning and thunder, the storm seemed to be heading toward the airport. Finally, even though the water was high enough to float the car, the Robo slowed when he saw through the murk the A-Team rendezvous point.

But suddenly, flash, bang, boom. A lightning bolt struck the car. Emily felt the Robo pulling her out just before she blacked out.

When she awoke, she didn't know how long she had been unconscious, but she knew from the A-Teamer hovering above and the Robo sitting across the aisle that they were safely airborne.

The A-Teamer said,

Ah, Miss Emily, so glad you wake up. We halfway back. You tell Electra-C what happened when we get there. Until then, rest easy."

Emily did just that.

Chapter 4

June 2342

"A Parade of Big Questions"

Emily took two days to summarize her trip before contacting Electra-C. When finished, Electra-C said,

"You should be pleased with what you accomplished, but why do you look puzzled?"

"You said that I was created for a purpose. Is that why I survived the lightning bolt?"

"Not even the Singularity can control the weather. Fate was responsible for your surviving the strike, and in the parlance of modern physics, Heisenberg's uncertainty principle says so. It states that there is a fundamental limit to the precision with which certain pairs of physical properties of a particle, like position and momentum, or energy and time, can be known simultaneously. The more accurately one property is measured, the less accurately the other can be known. But don't dwell on modern physics for very long. It has become more like a religion than a science."

Erika had more questions.

"You also said that most people aren't created for a purpose other than to go on living. That's why people are predisposed to have offspring and seek intimate relations. If that's the case, life seems so pointless. Maybe people should just commit suicide. Why am I thinking this way?"

"Because you are like your predecessor, more philosophical than materialistic. And I'll give you the same advice I gave her. Don't ponder life's big questions for too long. Find things you want to do that make you happy and keep busy with them. Why not talk with Lily and decide what you'll do next?"

Lily had been standing close by during the discussion, so she spoke as soon as Electra-C's avatar vanished.

"Life's big questions take us into philosophy and religion. I helped Erika explore these topics, and I think you should listen to my review."

After finishing it twenty minutes later, Emily asked a pertinent question.

"So, now what? How can I extend it?"

"Why not use your searching skills to delve into New Age Religion, and then have Professor Chen refer you to the University's school of theology?"

"Wonderful idea. I'll start right now."

Emily spent the remainder of the day learning about New Age religion, which she summarized before going to bed.

New Age religion is an approach to spirituality that's a broad and diverse collection of beliefs and practices, often described as a movement rather than a formal religion. It emphasizes personal experience, self-discovery, and spiritual growth, drawing from Eastern mysticism, Western occultism, and even elements of traditional religions. A key aspect is the belief in a divine force within oneself and the potential for individual transformation and enlightenment.

Several religions that label themselves "New Age" and distinguish themselves from traditional religions by believing in one or more of the following. Astrology, the belief that celestial bodies impact human affairs. Reincarnation, the belief that a soul, upon death, can begin a new life in a new body.

Psychics, the belief that some individuals possess extrasensory perception or the ability to communicate with spirits. Spiritual Energy, the belief that spiritual energy can reside in physical objects or locations.

According to a recent PEW survey, 49% of Americans hold at least one of these beliefs, highlighting the widespread acceptance of certain New Age concepts even among those who identify with more traditional religions.

Whew, I've done enough for one day. Tomorrow, I'll build my forecast for trends and surprises in religion, which I'll use to entice Professor Chen's contact at the university's theology department.

Emily started her morning by first searching for summary information about the school's department.

The Divinity School is renowned for its critical and rigorous approach to the academic study of religion, encompassing diverse traditions and methodologies. It's a global leader in generating knowledge about the history, theology, beliefs, and practices of world religions.

OK, now I'll come up with a forecast that'll get their attention.

Emily spent the rest of the day building it and reviewed it one last time before going to bed.

Forecast Summary for Religions

United States: Key Trends

- Secularism continues to increase.

- The U.S. remains much more religious than other wealthy Western nations, with higher rates of belief in God, prayer, and church attendance.

- Christianity is still dominant, but its share is declining. Around thirty percent of Americans now identify with a religion, mainly Christian denominations.

- American religiosity is higher than in most developed countries, with only fifteen percent of their people viewing religion as "very important" in their lives.

- Evangelical and Pentecostal Christian denominations have the slowest decline, but overall religious identification (and especially mainline denominations) is declining as more people opt for spirituality outside organized religion.

- A significant segment of the traditional religions' churchgoers are switching to New Age Religion.

- The New Age movement is a broad collection of beliefs and practices rather than a single unified organization or dogma. However, some groups and ideas have gained significant popularity and influence.

Global Trends

- Religious affiliation outside the developed world remains high: fifty percent of people globally identify with a religion. Hinduism, Buddhism, and Islamism dominate.

Some Surprises for Religions in the U.S.

- The government might ban religions that disagree with its politics.
- Churches might hire armed guards to protect churchgoers.
- The New Age movement might position itself as the alternative to science-and-technology-driven secularism.

When Emily called the next morning, Professor Chen dominated the conversation at the start.

"When I explained to one of our corporate partners what your forecasting service does, he said he wants to meet you in person. His company, the Sustainability Farming Solution,

is located in Austin, Texas. I'll give you his phone number and Email address."

"This is great news. I'll contact him. And may I explain why I called?"

"Of course."

"Would you give me a contact at the School of Divinity? I have a forecast they might like to see."

"What a novel idea, forecasting religion. I know just the person. Here's the name and number, but give me a day to tell her."

"OK, and thanks."

After ending the call, Emily knew it was time to call Electra-C and spoke as soon as the avatar appeared.

"It's time to plan a trip to some EU contacts and a potential client in Texas."

"Your A-Team can handle both locations on one trip. Just tell them you want to travel fast. And you know how to travel light, but on some future trips, you'll want to pack a Cyborg Suit and Helmet."

"What is that?"

"It's the uniform that soldiers and astronauts wear for protection from weapons, radiation, and germs. The suit and gloves feature built-in sensors and strength amplifiers, and the helmet provides a view in all directions and a range of frequencies. You'll be almost as indestructible as your Robos."

"How do I get one?"

"Ask the A-Team to get it for you."

"I'll contact them as soon as I line up the travel dates."

"Excellent, now carry on and contact me if you need my assistance."

After the avatar vanished, Emily said to Lily, who was standing nearby.

"It's time to gear up for another trip."

Chapter 5
July 2342

"Traveling Fast and Light "

Emily and her A-Team contact had adjusted nicely to each other's styles. Her contact summarized the details after Emily explained where she wanted to go.

"Ah, Miss Emily, we fly you and Robo from Pequot Lab first to Riga, capital of Latvia, for meeting with Baltic states, and for sightseeing pleasure, we give him nice driving route. Then, we fly to Austin, Texas, for meeting with potential client. You have plenty time on flight to put on Cyborg-Suit we get for you. Robo know nice driving route to client. And then, we fly back to Pequot Lab. You like?"

"Wonderful. We'll be ready when you pick us up."

Emily spent the first hour of the flight getting acquainted with her Cyborg-Suit.

The hard-shell exterior is surprisingly light, and its haptic gloves give me a sense of touch that lets me pick up and manipulate objects. When I put on the helmet, the virtual world I'm in mirrors the 3-D one.

I don't think I'll need it for my meeting in Riga, but it's better to practice now so I'm ready when it's needed.

Afterward, Emily used her laptop to search for background information on these Baltic countries.

Lithuania, Latvia, and Estonia share a complex history marked by periods of independence, foreign rule, and ultimately, a return to self-governance. Initially inhabited by various Baltic and Finnish tribes, the Teutonic Knights, Poland, Sweden, and the Russian Empire took over. Following World War I, they briefly gained independence, but the

Soviet Union annexed them in 1940. After decades under Soviet rule, they reasserted their independence in 1991.

I can put together a meeting presentation that'll impress everyone there.

Emily and the Robo used the two hours before the meeting to tour Riga.

I see in the early morning sunlight that the traffic and roads are like those of a modern, bustling city. The stunning architecture gives the capital its nickname—the Paris of the East. And the Old Town area has well-preserved medieval buildings, cobblestone streets, and picturesque squares. Judging from the museum and theater district, it has to be a cultural center. What a wonderful place to live.

The guard at the security desk escorted Emily to the conference room at 10 a.m. She saw a male-female pair of diplomatic and military types seated on three of the four sides of a large table. In typical European thoroughness, each pair had tent cards giving the names and countries. The diplomat from Latvia rose to greet her while Emily sat on the unoccupied side. After making introductions, the Latvian lady turned the meeting over to Emily, who distributed copies of her presentation before starting.

"I thought you might like to see what my forecasting service can do, so I've assembled some graphs that plot over time what it forecast and what Russia actually did. The first one shows that it forecast ahead of time Russia's aggressive moves."

Emily paused for comments that she knew would come from the military types.

"If the countries they attacked had known ahead of time what Russia would do, they could have had their defenses ready, and other EU countries would have helped."

"That's the idea. Now, look at the next graph. It shows our forecast of what Russian propaganda would say compared to what actually happened."

This time, the diplomatic types commented.

"The Kremlin never tells its true intentions. Can your software analyze what the Russian president says and then predict what he and the government will do?"

"Yes, and now look at the third graph. It shows our forecast of new Russian weapons compared to when they reached the Russian military."

Both military and diplomatic types commented.

"Knowing this would help us plan our military budget, and it would help our fellow allies."

Emily's expression mirrored her cautionary note.

"That's right, but don't expect the United States to pitch in until its government adjusts to the new realities."

A spirited discussion continued for another ninety minutes before the Lithuanian diplomatic lady ended the meeting.

"We'll certainly want you to run more forecasts for us. How will you do that?"

"Call me or tell the EU office in DC what you want. I'll run them for each country separately."

"What great service. We'll keep in touch."

Emily divided the flight time to Austin between learning about Austin and researching what might interest the Sustainability Solution Company.

The city's on the eastern edge of the Texas hill country. It's a center for computer chip manufacturing and is also known for its vibrant entertainment, art, culture, and the Texas Longhorns football team. The University of Texas main campus is in the center of the town. We'll have to drive around before meeting my potential client.

Finding many sustainability options, Emily selected several that would make a nice package.

Enclosed facilities for growing protein or veggies, and outdoor facilities for harnessing wind or solar energy make sense. Cultured meat made from animal cells grown in a lab-like setting is one source of protein, as are some types of insects. Both can be grown in fully enclosed vertical structures to conserve space, and these structures work for some vegetables, where twenty-four-hour daylight and controlled temperature and humidity assure bumper crops.

And for energy, solar panels on vertical structures surrounded by windmills make sense. I can compare my ideas with those of my potential client.

The Robo's tour through Austin showed a blend of high-tech industry and Texas charm. Emily strode to the front door of a typical middle-class house in a neighborhood on the fringe of the city after the Robo parked out front at 11 a.m.

Wearing a Texas-friendly smile and offering a firm handshake, Hank Katchem matched Hollywood's image of a Texan: big, strong-looking, and talking with a pleasant Texas drawl.

"Well, howdy, little lady. C'mon in outta the hot sun and tell me all about your forecasting stuff."

Hank escorted her to a table in the family room.

"Can I get ya something to drink?"

"Ice water's fine for me."

"OK, I'll be right back. I'm gonna get me a Coke, but if we had all our business talked out, I'd be sippin a beer."

Five minutes later, Emily began talking about sustainability forecasting that might entice Hank.

"From what Professor Chen told me about your company, I can think of three types of sustainability where my forecasts might fit. The first is energy sustainability via vertical solar panel structures surrounded by windmills. My forecasting models predict both short and long-term weather, so you'll know when to turn off the equipment to prevent damage. They'll also say when to build new energy farms because of climate change."

Emily paused for Hank to comment.

"Hmm, that's got possibilities for my combo windmill and solar panel farm. What else?"

"How about better and more cost-effective protein sources. Long ago, Austin cattle ranches provided a lot of protein, but today we know that cattle need a lot of land and energy, produce temperature-warming methane, and yield fatty protein loaded with feed hormones. You could switch to cultured meat grown in lab-like settings, or to a self-contained vertical insect farm, where there are no worries about the weather, invasive bacteria, or viruses."

"Tarnation, I've got one that grows cockroaches. How could your forecasts help?'

"They could alert you to the latest vertical farm structures and advances in types and methods of insect harvesting. And the same applies to my third type of farm, vertical vegetable structures. It uses enclosed towers that have twenty-four-seven lighting and water control."

"I got me one ah them too. How about we take a tour after lunch?"

"I'd like that, and I'll wear my Cyborg Suit for protection. You and your farmhands could use it when danger arises, such as closing down windmills and panels when a storm approaches, being exposed to bacteria, viruses, or poisonous gases, and climbing around in vertical farms. I'll explain how it works while we're driving."

Emily admitted that Hank's barbecued ribs served with fries and coleslaw tasted better than most of her meals before saying,

"Eating insects is an acquired taste I don't have."

"Little lady, I'm with you on that."

Emily's suit impressed Hank, and by the time they reached the windmill farm, she had answered all his questions. He and his manager watched as she climbed to the top of a windmill and then jumped onto a solar panel tower before descending effortlessly.

She did much the same on the vertical vegetable tower, and from there, Hank drove them to his insect farm. He explained how his design differed from a tower. When they arrived, Hank introduced her to the manager and explained what she was wearing. When Hank finished, the fellow said,

"We could use it around here when operating some of the heavy equipment or climbing into the underground silos. That's where we breed the insects. Lemme take you on a tour."

He started at the garage that housed the machinery and vehicles used for transporting insects to the protein processing area. Then he took them to a row of underground silos. His description matched the impressive structures she was staring at.

"Each silo stands ten feet above the ground, has a diameter of fifteen feet, and goes forty feet down. I use a computer to control the interior environment, and the clear plastic hinged dome on the top makes it easier to see in and is light enough to unseat. All you do is turn the wheel on the top. Why don't you climb the steps to unseat it and peer in?"

Emily said,

"I will," before putting her helmet and gloves back on.

She climbed the steps and had the dome flipped open a minute later, before she leaned forward to peer in, but as she did, a sudden gust of wind upset her balance. She tried leaning backward, but her center of gravity shifted forward, and she plunged headfirst into the silo.

Hank and his manager stared mutely at one another until Hank came to his senses and shouted,

"What do we do now?"

"You stay here. I'll get some rope from the shed."

He returned with three coils that they tied together, but before the manager could climb in, Emily climbed out. Hank hugged her even before she could take off her helmet, and after doing so, she said,

"The cockroaches cushioned some of the impact, but my Cyborg Suit kept me injury-free."

"Tell ya what, I'll sign your contract if you tell me how to get a couple of suits that'll fit my manager and me."

"Now that's a deal that'll fit both of us."

Chapter 6

August 2342

"Getting to know Me "

"How soon can you meet with me and some of our leading Matriarchate candidates in my Washington office? We've developed approaches to some campaign issues that'll make voters like us better than they'll like the incumbents."

The tone of Emily's voice hid her surprise as best she could.

"Let me check my schedule… will 8 a.m. next Friday work?"

"Yes."

"Good, and if you tell me what campaign issues are top priority, I can prepare a report explaining what the other parties' approaches are likely to be, and what you can use to counter them and attract voters."

"Here are the top ones—gerrymandering congressional districts in several states ahead of what their state constitutions allow, climate change, sustainability, and helping EU countries defend themselves against Russian aggression."

"I'll come prepared. And that gives me an idea. I can write newsletters that your candidates can use in their campaign speeches."

"Erika Kincaid used to do that for us if we covered her costs. Can you do that too?"

"I'm a good wordsmith. We can talk more about it after you see my reports. See you next Monday."

Erika turned to Lily as soon as the call ended.

"It's time for the A-Team to set up another trip. I won't need my Cyborg Suit, and one Robo should be plenty."

"And why not add Chicago to the itinerary? You can chat with Professor Chen regarding your trip to Hank's sustainability farms, and then with the contact she gave you at the school's Department of Divinity before going to Washington."

"That's a great idea. I'll call them right now."

Two hours later, Emily explained the itinerary.

"I'll meet with Professor Chen on Monday at 9 a.m. and with the person my Divinity contact lined up the next day at the same time."

"That leaves the weekend open. What do you plan to do?"

"Prepare for the Chicago meetings. And on Friday night, I'll

do something that's caught my attention, speed dating. It's a popular and safe way to meet members of the sex you're interested in."

"Are you interested in dating?"

"Not really, but I want to see how going to a speed dating club feels. After viewing some websites, I don't think I'll need my Cyborg Suit, but I will pack high heels and something sexy. I've even found the club I'll go to, the Superior Speed-Dating Club. I'll go there Friday evening and have the A-Team get me to Chicago by Sunday evening. And I can use my free time in Chicago for whatever comes up."

Now sitting across from the Senator, Emily made the first move.

"Here's the report I promised you. You'll see I added two additional issues that worry the public—the President dispatching the National Guard to cities even though the city or state officials don't want them, and the CIA searching the homes of presidential appointees who have fallen out of favor."

Senator Windstein skimmed the document for five minutes before saying,

"Your writing is as good as your predecessor's. Our congresswomen will have no trouble understanding your bullet points. I'll hand out copies at the start of the meeting before making opening remarks. Let's go to the conference room now."

On the way, she gave the document to her secretary, who would make copies. Once there, she had Emily sit next to her after each had poured a cup of coffee. Twenty minutes later, after the congresswomen had filled the chairs and cups, the Senator stood to start the meeting.

"Please take from the stack on the table a copy of the report prepared by Emily Kimball, who's sitting next to me. She is our replacement for Erika Kincaid."

Senator Windstein continued a minute later.

"The unknown person, organization, or country that blew up the White House and Capitol two years ago did what many people wanted but no one could. That person provided an opportunity for the American people to redeem the best of our nation by putting in place a new set of senators and representatives who would work for the people, not the old political system. The people made a good start by electing some of our new party's candidates, but the old parties still hold more power than the people want. All congresspeople face elections this year, as do I."

Senator Windstein paused for comments.

One congresswoman said,

"This report tells how our party can use the issues identified to convince people to vote for us. Why don't we talk about it and maybe come up with others?"

"You read my mind. That's what I was going to say."

Emily took notes until Senator Windstein ended the meeting at noon.

"Thanks to all of you for contributing. Please use the report to your advantage. I'll be doing the same. We have almost three months until the election, so I'll call another meeting near the end of September. Try to make things happen in our favor between now and then."

Emily and the Senator continued sitting, saying nothing until everyone had left. Then, she turned to Emily.

"I want you to be part of my campaign team. What will it take to make that happen?"

"By that, do you mean for me to prepare more reports and write campaign speeches?"

"And also meet with my team and me in NYC."

"Just tell me when, and I'll adjust my schedule."

"Wonderful. I'll let you know next week when and where…"

The Robo drove around the Georgetown commercial district, where most speed dating clubs were located, and Emily decompressed from the meeting's stress by sitting in the back seat and surfing for information on speed dating in DC.

Everyone attending will be in their twenties or thirties, have professional careers, be well-groomed, and sharp dressers. Some guys might be sporting the bald power look, and those with beards will have them neatly trimmed.

The muscular look is in for the guys, but for the gals, it's trim and thin. They won't eat dinner or anything from the snack table during the meet and mingle session, because that could cause tummy bloat or something stuck between the teeth. I'll stick to one drink, and I'll hold on to it all night. That'll keep my hands from waving around or a fellow from grabbing them while chatting me up. And I won't have to say much. Guys love to brag about themselves, so all I have to do is listen insouciantly.

Driving past the club, the Robo said,

"The neighborhood looks safe. I will find a self-parking lot that's close enough for you to walk while I stay in the car. Keep your cell phone, so I'll know your location, and you can call me if you need assistance."

"You're as thorough as Electra-C, but I should be fine tonight. Speed dating clubs are safe, and I can't imagine the area having much crime. The streets and sidewalks are trash-free, and all the storefronts have that just-painted-and-decorated look."

"What do you want to do now?"

"Keep driving around while I continue unwinding. At about six, stop at a fast-food place so I can change into my date-club clothes and high heels. Then find a place to park so I can walk to the club and get there for mixing and mingling, which starts at seven."

As soon as Emily entered, even the guard at the door added to the upscale atmosphere. She did notice the tiny bulge of a gun under his tuxedo jacket, but she thought few others would. After checking her ID and purse, he said,

"You're not a member, but if you join right now, you'll get a thirty-dollar discount, which takes the cost of admission down to what members pay."

After he handed her a ticket good for one drink, she said,

"If I enjoy the evening, perhaps I'll join when I leave."

"Well, if you do, I'll still give you the discount."

Emily ordered a zero-proof No-Groni and then mingled with the growing crowd, which matched her expectations. The lights flickered at 8 p.m. Then, the crowd listened to one of the hosts.

"Tonight, we'll have the ladies sit for the first two hours so the gentlemen can introduce themselves, and then we'll have the men sit until we say goodnight at midnight. So, let the meeting begin."

Time melted away for Emily as a steady stream of fellows chatted her up, and she maintained her suave but silent appearance by nodding occasionally and never smiling. When the host asked the men to sit, Emily retreated to the ladies' lounge. As soon as she entered, one girl primping in the mirror turned to her and said,

"You're not a member, are you? I'd remember if you were. You'd be tough competition."

Emily smiled before entering a stall. She came out a half-hour later and began sitting with guys she thought were sexy, asking and answering questions, but neither smiling nor giving any hints that she found them desirable. When the host announced it was time to leave, she sauntered out with the crowd, which disappeared into the night.

Hearing footsteps behind, Emily glanced over her shoulder soon after turning a corner and saw two fellows heading her way. When she increased her pace, they did too, so she started running, but the high heels slowed her down and made her stumble when she reached the parking lot. She hit her head and then rolled onto her back, unable to get up.

The two fellows trotted up, and each unzipped his fly before the taller guy said,

"You shouldn't have dissed on us. We were merely talking and asking harmless questions. Now, it's our turn to diss on you."

But before they could, Emily's Robo grabbed each by the shoulder and flung them to the pavement. After watching them run, he carried Emily to the car. He put her down before saying,

"Do you need medical attention?"

"No, just drive someplace so I can change into my travel clothes. Then drive around while I sleep in the backseat."

When sunrise came, Emily awoke feeling both starved from not eating for twelve hours and stiff from scrunched-up sleeping. After buying a mix-and-match deal at a McDonald's drive-thru, she called the A-Team to hasten the flight to Chicago after gobbling the first.

"I need to get there sooner, and I need a hotel room downtown. I'll be there for three days, so make sure it has a parking garage. The Robo and I will stay in the room."

"Ah so, Miss Emily. We handle."

Emily spent the rest of Saturday preparing for her meeting with Professor Chen, and she used a workstation to print the report.

She arrived at the Professor's office on Monday at 9 a.m. After the typical ice-breaking chit-chat, Professor Chen said,

"Most sustainability farms are for energy, vegetables, and protein, but there's fourth type that we call mining. The economy needs resources like copper, iron, and rare earths. They're dug from the earth or recycled. Some experts talk about getting them from other planets or asteroids, but that's infeasible today. However, seabed mining is happening right now, and the technology keeps improving."

"I never thought that way about mining, but you're right. And my report on the public's concern about sustainability connects with it. Here's your copy."

Chen read for five minutes before commenting.

"Yes, Americans remain concerned about sustainability and environmental issues, with many actively seeking sustainable products and expecting companies and governments to act more responsibly on climate change. While political and economic factors sometimes influence priorities, surveys show consistency about people's concerns for climate change and sustainability."

Emily nodded before saying,

"I'll add resource mining to the prompt when I run your next report. Is there anything else you'd like to talk about?"

"Not for today, but please keep in touch."

Emily and the Robo returned to the hotel, where she unwound by watching the local news.

Both the mayor and governor told Congress they don't need troops protecting the city. So, what does the President do? Goes on social media to call them incompetent. I'll mention this to Senator Windstein when I get home.

She spent the rest of the time preparing for tomorrow's meeting and surfing for information about Chicago until she needed a break. Then she walked to one of the city's iconic pizza restaurants for a mid-afternoon lunch. She had the extra slices wrapped and then did downtown sightseeing.

Many people are getting around on electric bikes that can be left anywhere for the next rider, but I'd rather walk. The downtown area is called the Loop because most of it is within a square formed by elevated train tracks. Most of the buildings are old and have been repurposed for new uses. The financial district runs north-south on LaSalle Street, which has the old-old Board of Trade Building at the south end. Its trading floor used to handle commodities like corn, soybeans, and pork bellies, but online AI-powered software has replaced it.

And the commercial district runs parallel to LaSalle along State and Wabash streets. Famous stores like Marshall Fields, Carson Pirie Scott, and Sears Roebuck had their own buildings at one time, but they've either been acquired by bigger chains or gone out of business. And downtown has the largest number of college students living in shared housing than any other major city. Chicago's a great place to live or work.

Emily spent the rest of the day until bedtime either watching the news or surfing for information on the trends in New Age religion so she could hold her own at tomorrow's meeting.

Emily gazed at the imposing church when she arrived at the First New Age Church of Chicago, located on the city's south side.

This must have been a Catholic church before the Chicago diocese downsized. I'll find out more after I get buzzed in.

She pressed the button, and seconds later a voice spoke.

"Are you Emily Kimball?"

"Yes, the University of Chicago's School of Divinity referred me to you."

"Wait inside after I buzz you in. I'll be right there."

Emily glanced at the stairway when she heard steps descending.

That's one attractive black female. She has to be at most in her mid-forties.

Emily matched her contact's warm smile when she said,

"Good morning, Emily. I'm Hope Masondo. Please follow me."

She followed to a tiny but tidy office and was now sitting across at a desk. Emily made the first comment to start the conversation.

"This is quite a building."

"Our church needed a bigger building, and we bought it when the diocese closed some of its parishes. We converted the rectory into offices and the convent into a shelter for the homeless or runaways."

"Did you always want to work in religion?"

"Far from it. My folks took me to church when I was in grade school. I liked the music and singing, but the Bible readings and sermons bored me. I could never sit still and listen for very long."

"So, what brought you here?"

"I worked in the legal department for several large corporations, but I found their relentless drive for ever more sales and profits by paying only lip service to ethics so disheartening. That's when I started searching online for alternative approaches to religion and came across the New Age movement. And the rest is what you see."

"So, what do you do?"

"I manage our website and blogging platform, help run the office for our pastor, and do some counseling."

"I know something about the New Age movement, but you know more. How would you summarize it?"

"New Age spirituality is a broad term describing a contemporary movement, not a traditional religion, that emphasizes individual spiritual growth and transformation through eclectic practices and beliefs. It's characterized by a rejection of traditional religious structures and doctrines, and a focus on personal experience and self-discovery."

Emily asked another question when Hope paused.

"Most religions in America are shrinking, but why is the New Age movement growing?"

"We offer personalized spiritual paths and online communities. Americans also like our focus on personal growth and self-improvement workshops. These ideas are gaining traction, particularly among the religiously unaffiliated, indicating a broader societal shift towards spiritual exploration outside traditional institutions. Younger generations in particular are embracing a "spiritual but not religious" identity, forming personal belief systems rather than committing to established faiths."

When Hope paused, Emily said,

"All that sounds good to me, but I've also read about increasing violence and shootings in churches. Has that ever happened here?"

"Once in a while, even though our message is better. We aren't immune to targeted violence from extremists or mentally challenged people. And we're a soft target with large gatherings of people in accessible places. Social unrest and political polarization lead to online radicalization. That's why we have surveillance cameras and discreetly post guards during services."

"How often do you hold them?"

"Tuesdays and Fridays at 8 p.m., and Sundays at 11 a.m. Why don't you come tonight?"

"I will, but I won't bother you. I'll just sit with the others in a pew."

Emily understood why a crowd came early when she did too.

People can grab a snack from the buffet table at the back while listening to a band play Christian rock music.

Emily took mental notes when the pastor began the service at 7 p.m.

He's talking about neighborhood outreach programs and how they connect to his in-house ones…now he's welcoming anyone who needs shelter to stay… and now he's explaining why the troubled world needs to be kinder and gentler, and how New Age religion can be part of the solution.

Emily liked what she was hearing, but yelling followed by gunfire erupted in the back. The pastor pointed to an exit behind him before shouting,

"Drop everything and follow me."

Emily fled with the crowd.

Her cell phone flashed 9:55 by the time she and the Robo entered their hotel room. When Emily turned on the news, the banner scrolling across the bottom said shots had been fired at a local church. Minutes later, a station writer handed the newscaster a bulletin.

"Police confirm that shots have been fired at the city's First New Age Church, and multiple injuries have been reported. Stay tuned for the latest developments."

Emily did so the next morning while packing for the flight. She finished ahead of any updates, so she flipped off the TV.

I've had enough excitement on this trip. When I get home, I must tell Senator Windstein's campaign team about it, and another trip might be the best way to decide what else I want and need in the coming days. And I'll call Hope to make sure she's OK.

Chapter 7

September 2342

"The Novice Crime Stopper "

Emily's calls to the church went unanswered over the weekend, but she recognized Hope's voice when calling on Monday and said,

"Good morning, this is Emily Kimball. I was at the church when gunshots stopped the service. Your pastor reacted bravely by pointing to the safest way out, and the news I watched reported that people had been injured, but didn't say who. So, I'm calling to find out if you and your pastor are OK."

"Hello, Emily, and thanks for caring. I'm fine, but our pastor was among those injured. However, the bullet missed vital spots, so he's recovering."

"I'm relieved to hear that. What a terrifying event. Maybe you'll need more guards posted where potential perpetrators can see them."

"That's something we'll consider."

"Good. Well, I know you're extra busy today, so let's end the call so I'm out of your way."

"Please visit the next time you come to Chicago, and have a blessed day."

Going about her normal business for the rest of the day, Emily made progress thinking about future trips and what Senator Windstein might want, and in preparation for the next one, called the A-Team.

"Ah, Miss Emily, so glad you call. How may I assist?"

"I need to carry some sort of weapon on future trips. What would you recommend?"

"I know what you need. I get you can of Mace pepper spray and gun. Both easy to conceal in purse."

"I know almost nothing about guns. What kind?"

"I get Glock 43X pistol, two bullet magazines, extra bullets, and silencer."

"That seems like a lot of firepower. Do I need that much?"

"Good to plan ahead. I order if you say OK and send items."

"You're right. Please do. And I'll contact you when I have another trip in mind. Bye-bye."

Emily kept happily busy for the next couple of days. She considered calling Senator Windstein but decided to wait for her call, which came Thursday evening.

"How soon can you meet with me and my campaign team in New York City?"

"Let me check my calendar... how about Monday afternoon?"

"That's a go."

"Should I drive?"

"Don't. New York City's congestion is terrible. Take a train on Amtrak's Northeast Corridor to Grand Central Station and then ride the subway system."

"Is it safe?"

"There are guards posted everywhere, and you'll have plenty of fellow riders, so the answer's yes. Are you ready to jot down the directions?"

"Yes."

After doing so, Emily said,

"I'll be there as close to noon as I can. And what can you tell me to help prepare?"

"It's better to wait until you get here. My campaign team has all the details."

"Fair enough. Bye-bye until then."

Emily called the A-Team after the Senator ended the call.

"I need you to arrange a trip for me, Lily, and one Robo to the Pequot Reservation. We'll stay there over the weekend, and on Monday, the Robo will drive me to a train station so I can get to a meeting in New York City."

"Ah, so, we can do. We have car waiting, and if weapons we order come before we take you, we bring them too."

"And if they don't, you can send them to the Pequot Reservation's Deus Lab, because I plan to stay there until I'm ready to fly back to Bern."

"We can do that."

Emily used the weekend to rest but also to check train and subway schedules. She chose her departure station and time that her Robo would use to get her to campaign headquarters by noon on Monday.

After Emily identified herself to the campaign worker controlling admittance, he took her to a conference room where five people sat around the table and said,

"Here's Emily Kimball, right on time."

Staying seated, Senator Windstein pointed to the empty chair next to her and continued looking at Emily while saying,

"Let me make some comments before I turn the discussion over to Jonah Cohen. We've identified a problem that I believe Emily can solve, and I'll start by asking her a question. Do you know what a crime stopper is?"

"Uh, no. Please tell me."

"Officially, it's an organization that links citizens to law enforcement agencies. The citizens provide information about criminal activity to the crime stopper organization, and it passes the information to the appropriate law enforcement agency for investigation. If the information leads to an arrest, the tipster receives a reward. Well, we want Emily to be our very own anonymous crime stopper who digs up information about specific candidates who might defeat our Matriarchate party candidates, investigates these opposition candidates, and if she uncovers incriminating data, turns it over to the press and the law enforcement agencies to expose their criminal activity. That should get our candidate elected. Emily's very smart, and I expect her to understand what I just said, so unless she says she doesn't, Jonah will dig into the details."

After Emily gave a thumbs up, Jonah took over, speaking directly to her.

"So, here's the deal. Our candidates are putting the campaign issues you identified on their websites and in their brochures. They also hype them in their speeches. But the opposing candidate copies them and does the same, which neutralizes our position. Got that?"

"Yes, keep going."

"But our candidates can't badmouth the other side regarding this. That would turn off the voters. That's why we need you to be our anonymous crime stopper by digging up the dirt and letting the press and the police throw it. How does that sound?"

"I haven't eaten since breakfast. Do you have something I can snack on and wash down with a Coke?"

The Senator replied,

"We should all do that, and we'll leave Emily alone until she's ready to continue."

Emily mused about what type of crime stopper she would become while sipping a Coke and nibbling on a cheese-cream-covered bagel. Her thoughts snapped into focus just before Jonah called the meeting to order.

Jonah's smart, but I'm smarter. I know how to do what he wants, but I'd better tell him diplomatically. After all, I'm on his team.

When Jonah asked if she was ready, she smiled and said,

"Eating something helped me figure out what I can do for you and your candidates. No matter how many opposing candidates you want me to investigate, I should be able to handle up to five simultaneously, and I'll need a lot of information. Let me describe what it includes. OK for me to proceed?"

"Go on."

For each Matriarch candidate, give me their name, state, and the position for they're running for. Then give me the main opponent's name, party affiliation, and close campaign associates. And after that, tell me what type of crime you think they're committing and the laws they're breaking. The last piece of information is a list of people who would like to tattle on them. I'll then use all this to start digging into the opponent's past and present. How does that sound?"

Jonah glanced around the table for a volunteer, but no one spoke, which forced Jonah to say,

"Like you're ahead of even me. Your pieces of info include all I could think of, but have you thought about where you'll look to dig up the dirt?"

"There are only two places, but they cover everything, online and in the 3-D world."

"I'm ahead of you on this one. Only in the 3-D world for the dirt. You know why?"

"No. Please tell me."

"Lawbreakers are even more concerned than politicians about information leaking out that would tell their true intentions or what they're really gonna do, so they never talk or put incriminating details online. They do all the critical stuff face-to-face where surveillance can't eavesdrop. So even though you're supposed to be a crackerjack online surfer, don't bother looking online."

"You've just saved me a lot of time. I'll try to find any dirt the tattlers might have by looking in the real world. And here's my list of the criminal categories that anything I find will be important to voters: drug trafficking, illegal immigration, illegal gambling, child pornography, looting the financial assets of private citizens, and home burglary. What would you like to add?"

Senator Windstein broke in before Jonah could.

"I've heard enough. It's time we pick our top five candidates and build for Emily all the tattlers and their potential crime categories. Jonah, you take over from here. I have to leave for DC. Get the team to build it before Emily leaves."

Jonah waited for the Senator to leave before saying,

"OK, our top candidates will have to come from big-population states where the crime categories Emily chose are rampant. We'll start building the list after a ten-minute break."

Jonah ended the brainstorming session at 5 p.m.

"We are done. Emily's got her list, and now it's time for her to start digging. We must now pretend this meeting never happened, and Emily will never contact us again. So, everyone, go home."

Saying nothing, Emily was the first to leave, and she used the train ride home to think about what she would do tomorrow.

By the time the train pulled into her stop, the Robo was waiting, so she climbed into the back and pondered the day.

I enjoyed every minute. I learned a lot, sharpened my skills, and now I know what to do starting first thing tomorrow.

Chapter 8

September 2342

"On the Hunt"

At breakfast the next morning, Lily placed a box on the dining table before saying,

"The A-Team delivered this after you left for New York City. They didn't tell me what's in it, and I didn't ask."

"It contains some self-protection items I'll take on future trips. We'll open it as soon as I finish my bowl of Fiber-One cereal sprinkled with raisins."

Emily used a knife to slice the foot-long piece of tape that kept the box top shut before putting its contents on the table and then saying,

"Do you know what these are?"

"Two cans of Mace plus a gun and its attachments."

Emily inspected the items and figured out how to connect them.

"This is a Glock 43X, a couple of magazines, plenty of extra bullets, and a silencer. Let's go outside for target practice."

Using empty Coke cans for targets, both Emily and Lily had done enough shooting to handle the gun, so she now turned her attention to what she had initially planned to do: rewrite the list from yesterday's meeting. Two Cokes and three hours later, she read the document.

HUNTING LIST

Matriarchate Party Candidate: Coretta Brown State: Illinois Position being Sought: Congresswoman (Wants to unseat Incumbent)

- Main Opponent: Serenity Harris
- Party: Democratic Party
- Close Campaign Associates: **CURRENTLY UNKNOWN**
- Crimes and Laws Opponent might be breaking: Child Porn
- Potential Tattlers: **CURRENTLY UNKNOWN**

Matriarchate Party Candidate: Jose Perez

State: Texas   Position being Sought: Senator (Wants to unseat Incumbent)

- Main Opponent: Juan Garcia
- Party: Republican Party
- Close Campaign Associates: **CURRENTLY UNKNOWN**
- Crimes and Laws Opponent might be breaking: Illegal Immigration
- Potential Tattlers: **CURRENTLY UNKNOWN**

Matriarchate Party Candidate: Maria Gomez

State: California Position being Sought: Congresswoman (Wants to unseat Incumbent)

- Main Opponent: Jacqueline Boyd
- Party: Democratic Party
- Close Campaign Associates: **CURRENTLY UNKNOWN**
- Crimes and Laws Opponent might be breaking: Home Burglary, Financial Looting
- Potential Tattlers: **CURRENTLY UNKNOWN**

Matriarchate Party Candidate: Maria Sanchez State: Florida Position being Sought: Congressman (Wants to unseat the Incumbent)

- Main Opponent Name: Diego Lopez
- Party: Guardian Party
- Close Campaign Associates: **CURRENTLY UNKNOWN**
- Crimes and Laws Opponent might be breaking: Drug Trafficking
- Potential Tattlers: **CURRENTLY UNKNOWN**

Matriarchate Party Candidate: Angela Windstein

State: New York Position being Sought: Senator (Wants to be Re-Elected)

- Main Opponent Name: Hunter Bentley. Currently a three-term Congressman.
- Party: Democratic Party
- Close Campaign Associates: **CURRENTLY UNKNOWN**
- Crimes and Laws Opponent might be breaking: Prostitution
- Potential Tattlers: **CURRENTLY UNKNOWN**

I call it my hunting list for an obvious reason—I'll use it to find people who might snitch on main opponents. And I can find them only by traveling to their cities and then becoming an anonymous crime stopper. I have only two months to find them and collect information that I can turn into a press release. I'll plan my travel itinerary while running.

Returning an hour later, she jotted down what she had come up with.

Hunting Travel Plan

I now have a story to tell. So,

- I'll visit Chicago first, because I can tell it at the New Age Church.
- Then I'll adjust the story and tell it on another trip that'll include Houston and Los Angeles.
- Then, I'll take a final trip that'll include both Miami and New York City.
- I'll have the A-Team set up each trip for one Robo and me, and the A-Team will have a car waiting at the airport.

When Emily called the A-Team to say that she and her Robo wanted to arrive early Wednesday morning in Chicago, her regular contact said,

"Ah Miss Emily, we can do. Hope you enjoy time in Chicago. We fly you back when you say. Have good day."

When the Robo drove her to the church, Emily talked to a counselor other than Hope, so her identity would be unknown.

When he asked what help she needed, Emily began telling her story.

"I'm a crime victim. Do you hold meetings for victims to gather and support one another?"

"We're holding one tonight that'll be run by one of my associates, so please join us."

"I'll try, but if I can't make it, are there other South-Side churches that hold similar meetings?"

"Let me give you the names and addresses of several."

Sitting silently among the attendees who occupied only the first three rows of pews, Emily listened for anything the attendees said that might suggest they were victims of child pornography. Two youngish Black females seemed likely. Emily started speaking to them in a hushed voice during the break.

"I've been victimized by a guy who films child porn. I feel so ashamed that he filmed my daughter and me, but I needed the money, and I made sure he didn't hurt her too much. Has anything like that ever happened to you?"

They gawked at Emily, reluctant to answer until one finally said,

"I needed money, so I let him take a video of me with another guy, but I would never use my daughter as you did."

Emily saved herself from further embarrassment by saying,

"I'm sorry I bothered you," and then hurried away.

Undeterred, Emily began visiting other churches the next morning. After learning that all three had support-group meetings for crime victims, she prioritized them according to date and would attend the one for this evening.

The woman counselor ran the meeting like yesterday's. Emily spotted a young Black female who might have been a child porn victim, and during the break, approached her.

"I don't mean to intrude, but it's possible we can help one another. Can I explain how in private?"

The young woman licked her bottom lip while sizing Emily up from top to bottom before saying,

"OK."

When they walked far enough away from the others, Emily launched her story.

"I've been victimized by an amateur guy who films child porn. I feel so ashamed that I let him film my younger daughter and me, but I needed the money, and I made sure he didn't hurt her too much. Has anything like that ever happened to you?"

The woman pulled back for only a second or two before leaning in.

"Yeah. Just change 'guy' to 'lady' and you've got my story. How can we help each other?"

"How'd you like to get your money back and maybe put her out of business?"

"Tell me more."

"If you set up a meeting with her for both of us, we can make it happen."

"What'll I tell her?"

"Here's your story—you want to do another video because you need more money, and you'll bring another girl who wants to do the same. You and this new girl want to hold a meet-and-greet with you, and if it's looking good, we'll set a date for making the videos. That should do it. Just be cool on the call."

"I can do that. Then what?"

"If she agrees, we'll just act naturally when we get there."

"You're sure this'll work?"

"Trust me. I'll drive us to your place, and you make the call."

The girl peered into the car when Emily walked them to it and opened the rear door.

"Whoa, who the hell is that?"

"Our protection in case things go badly."

Emily climbed in and then said,

"Hop in."

Emily's ruse worked. They would meet in the basement of the lady's house, which served as her filming studio.

Emily spent the entire time until the meeting collecting what she needed and rehearsing what she would say and do. The meeting went according to plan, and when the lady bragged,

"I've got some very important people who buy my videos,"

Emily sprang the trap by removing her hidden camera.

"I'm going to add what you're now going to tell us about these VIPs." Emily pointed her Glock before the lady could do anything, and she started recording as soon as everyone settled down.

"OK, OK, how about I give you money?"

Emily looked at the girl, who said,

"I want five hundred, right now."

"You got it."

Emily said,

"We'll all walk to where you stash it."

Emily kept filming. After the lady paid the money, Emily said,

"Now tell me about your VIPs."

"Get this, a guy calls me every month or so. He's not the VIP, but says he works for this district's congressman, who just so happens to be a woman. I'm too busy trying to survive to follow politics, so I don't ask who she is, and he doesn't tell me her name, but he keeps on talking. He says sometimes she's in a video molesting the kids. And then—" Emily cut him off.

"If you give me a copy of a video she's in, I won't have the police bust you."

"Follow me."

Fifteen minutes later, Emily said,

"I've seen enough. It's time to go."

The Robo drove them to the young girl's home, and before he unlocked the doors, Emily said,

"So, now I've got your address, but please tell me your name and phone number, and I'll write them down."

Emily did that two minutes later. The girl exhaled slowly, pushed the door open, and walked away as if in slow motion, never looking back. Emily's car disappeared into the darkness.

Emily had more to do that evening. First, she made a backup copy of the recording, which she sealed in an envelope along with a note:

> You're the only TV station I'm giving this recording to.
>
> You'll shock some South-Side Chicago voters because it reveals something evil about a congresswoman who wants to get reelected. I'm putting the names, addresses, and phone numbers on the back of this note. These people know all about the recording. Call the guy, because he makes kiddie porn videos. Call the girl because she was a victim.

Then she addressed it: To an Investigative Political Reporter who wants to scoop all other local stations.

When sunrise woke her, Emily told the Robo to drive to local station WGN's recording studio. She jumped out, handed the envelope to the security guard, jumped back in, and the Robo drove away before he could say a word.

Emily knew it was time to call the A-Team.

"We're driving back to O'Hare Airport now. Please pick us up."

"We be there. Where we take you now?"

"Back to the Pequot Reservation."

"We be ready and contact you soon."

After the call ended, Emily told the Robo to stop at a McDonald's. When he did, she went into the restaurant for the McGriddles French Toast Breakfast. After devouring it, she told the Robo to drive the surface streets back to the airport while she would look at some Chicago neighborhoods while recapping the last twenty-four hours.

I'm becoming a dandy crime stopper. I can be even more devious than the crooks. And when I get back to the Deus Lab, I can use what I learned to prepare for the next trip.

The A-Team's call came early that afternoon. Once airborne, Emily slept all the way home.

Chapter 9

September 2342

"Two-Tattler Hunting"

Emily kept extra busy that weekend, adjusting her story while also searching the Internet for late-breaking political news from Chicago. Early the following week, she found what she had been waiting for when a WGN reporter said the following.

"This just in—one of our investigative reporters has just uncovered incriminating news about Serenity Harris, a Democratic candidate for Congress from the city's South Side. According to documented evidence, not only does she purchase child pornography videos, but she also participates in these acts of child molestation. We have contacted her for comments, but have not heard back. We will report details when they become available."

I can cross Chicago off my Hunting Travel Plan. Next up will be a trip covering both Houston and Los Angeles, so it's time to plan the details.

Completing it the next day, she contacted the A-Team. When her regular contact answered, Emily said,

"I want you to set up a trip for one Robo and me, similar to the last one. You'll fly us from the Pequot Lab to Houston's George Bush Intercontinental Airport, where there'll be a car waiting and a hotel reservation downtown. I'll contact you when we're ready to fly to LA Intercontinental Airport, where you'll have a car waiting and a hotel reservation near Hollywood. And after that, I'll contact you when I'm ready to fly back to the Pequot Lab."

"Ah, Miss Emily, we can do. When you leave?"

"Today's Tuesday, so pick us up early tomorrow morning."

"Very good. We be there."

Emily used some of the flight time to find helpful facts about Houston, summarizing to herself as she surfed the Web.

Houston's the center of America's oil patch. Every major international oil company has a headquarters downtown. The city ranks number four according to population, just behind Chicago's 3.5 million, which is only a little less than LA…but LA's only about half of New York's 8 million…and it's spread out, covering more than double the area of either Chicago or New York…I'll tell the Robo to drive us through the neighborhoods when time allows.

The Robo drove south on Interstate 45 for twenty miles to the Marriott Courtyard in downtown. Although traffic congestion seemed typical for a major metropolitan area, downtown was different from what she expected.

Although it has fewer tall buildings than Chicago, all the streets, sidewalks, and storefronts are spotless, and a futuristic trolley whisks people around. That must be why auto and foot traffic are light. Some of the streets are lined with greenery, and most restaurants have outdoor dining, but they won't be busy until the heat and humidity are less tropical. I'll do my sightseeing by car.

Emily spent the rest of the day planning her itinerary and practicing her story to fit her hunt for illegal immigration tattlers. Building on what she had learned at the New Age church in Chicago, she now had a list of places that might hold support group meetings for victims of illegal immigration.

The Robo waited in the car the next morning after driving her to The New Age Spiritual Center located in the Montrose area. Emily walked into a tidy building that matched the well-kept strip malls and modest homes and asked to speak with a counselor, who met with her in his office.

"And how may I help you, young lady?"

"Do you hold support group meetings for victims of crime?"

"Houston is like every big city. We have victims of all sorts, especially in illegal immigration. Why do you ask?"

"I have some friends who have relatives who wanted to work in the U.S., but they couldn't get immigrant visas. I thought I could help them by listening at a meeting."

"Oh, it'll come up, and you're in luck; the next one is tomorrow."

"I'll plan to come."

"Please do, and don't be shocked by what our attendees look like. Many come from Houston's East Side. That's where much of Houston's crime either originates or ends up."

"Thanks for letting me know."

Emily repeated her performance early that afternoon at the Houston Meditation Center, located in the University Place neighborhood, so named because of Rice University, which is sometimes referred to as one of the South's Ivy League schools.

She obtained similar results when chatting with a counselor, and this time the meeting would be held tonight, so she decided to attend.

Listening unobtrusively, she picked two reasonably dressed Mexican-Americans who might be potential tattler sources, and at the break pulled them aside before going into her act.

"I don't mean to intrude, but I think maybe we can help one another. Can I tell you more?"

The fellows glanced at each other before the older one said,

"We'll listen; go ahead."

"I have a friend who wants to bring a couple of relatives into the U.S., but they can't get immigration visas, so he wants to sneak them over the border, but he doesn't know how, so I said I'd help. I know how it's done, but I don't know anyone who smuggles people across the border. Can you introduce me to a person who arranges smuggling?"

He smirked before saying,

"Use the right word. You want us to introduce you to a coyote. I could, but I won't. Coyotes are suspicious. Doing that would put us in the crosshairs."

Emily frowned before saying,

"How about this? We can drive to where they are. All you have to do is point them out."

"What's in it for us?"

"I'll pay each of you five hundred on the spot, and I'll come back the next day and talk to them."

The fellows stepped a short distance away to huddle. When they returned, both wore smug smiles.

"That'll do. How about doing it tonight?"

"OK, meet me back here at 8 p.m."

The fellows were waiting when the Robo pulled up.

When they checked the car before getting in, the older guy pulled back after sizing up her partner.

"What is he? It doesn't look human."

"It's my protection in case things go haywire. Come on, get in. I'll sit between you. All you need to do is give directions and point to the coyotes if you see them. And let me guess, we'll be driving to Houston's East Side."

"What if they ain't?"

"We'll come back tomorrow."

After nodding to each other, the older guy nodded to Emily, and off they went. No one spoke until Emily asked a pointed question.

"Aren't coyotes targets for Immigration and Customs Enforcement agents? If so, they must have some way of getting out of a jam if they're caught. You think they have political connections?"

The older guy glanced sideways before saying with a sneer,

"All the smart ones do, and a coyote's boss has connections going even higher."

"That's what I thought." Emily didn't need to say anything else because the younger guy said,

"Shut up. We just entered the coyote zone."

Luck rode with them. After each pointed to their coyote, the Robo drove back to the Center. When she paid each by peeling crisp hundred-dollar bills off the roll she pulled from her purse, the older guy said,

"You ain't as clueless as I thought. Good luck."

Soon after each fellow opened their side door and slid out, the car glided away, while Emily began planning for the next day.

She used it to rehearse a script and procedure for convincing the coyotes to cooperate. She also found some shabby clothes for her Robo and herself. Then, she waited until twilight to launch the plan. The Robo cruised through one of the coyote zones, but Emily didn't spot the coyote, so rather than risk drawing attention, she told the Robo to cruise the other zone. By this time, darkness had closed in, and after spotting the coyote and his two guards stepping out of his car, Emily gave commands.

"Park close, and get ready to plant a tracker on his car as we walk past. Then, get ready to make a video of the coyote in action. I will too, using my hidden camera and microphone. And when I dive into action, get ready to pull me out if I need help. Let's go."

Their shabby clothes kept anyone from paying attention.

After filming for thirty minutes, Emily made her move. She pulled her pistol and yelled,

"I'm with ICE, and you're busted," but the two guards had other ideas. They charged her so quickly she had only enough time to shoot one in the foot before the other took her down with a flying tackle and began beating her, but the Robo stopped it. He ripped the guard off her and then body-slammed him onto the concrete before pounding him unconscious. He then grabbed the coyote, and Emily shouted,

"You're under arrest. I'm taking you to the station."

Although the crowd looked on while the Robo led him away, no one had time to spot their car, and when they had driven out of the zone, Emily said,

"I changed my mind. Let's drive to your place. Give my partner directions."

Emily talked further while her partner drove.

"How'd you like to avoid going to jail?"

He glanced furtively before replying.

"Who wouldn't? What do I gotta do?"

"Tell your big boss that someone you know wants to meet him. She has lots of friends who want to smuggle people across the border. If he agrees, we'll drive to his place."

"I've never been there, but I think it's his home."

"OK, just set up the time, and he can give you directions. And tell him I'll bring my partner."

"Lemme think." After several minutes, Emily told the Robo to stop.

"Are we close to your place?"

"If you turn left on the next side street, it's the fourth on the right."

"OK, get out here and when you've arranged the meeting. Give me your name, phone number, address, and the big boss's name and phone number. I'm giving you two days to call me. Otherwise, ICE agents will come knocking on your door."

Now it was the coyote's turn to ask a question.

"Are you really an ICE agent, and if so, it sounds like you're breaking the rules. And if you ain't, it sounds like you're up to blackmail. Which is it?"

"You don't need to know. Just follow the plan I've laid out, and you might not go to jail."

"OK, you win. I'll call you ASAP."

Emily did nothing the next day other than prepare. She confirmed the coyote's vital statistics; then rehearsed another story and contingency plan. When he called her mid-afternoon, she went into action. After placing a hidden camera, microphone, and pistol in her purse, she picked him up as the fiery sun was setting, and the Robo followed directions that took them to the upscale River Oaks neighborhood near the Galleria on Houston's west side. After the Robo parked in the driveway of a palatial home on a leafy side street, the coyote took them to his boss, who led them into a family room before starting the conversation.

"Why do you want to meet me? This coyote could have arranged for smuggling in the friends of your friends."

"I like doing business with the guy at or at least near the top. I'll pay you directly, and you can give Mr. Coyote whatever cut you want, but if my friends get caught, what can you do to help them?"

He smiled unctuously.

"They'll be in safe hands. I have Texas connections at the top."

"Good. I'll call to tell you how much I'm paying Mr. Coyote when he sets up what I want smuggled in."

He continued smiling while saying,

"I think we can conclude the meeting."

As everyone rose to leave, the coyote said,

"I got other things to talk about, so you drive away without me."

Emily said,

 "OK," and she and her Robo did so.

That triggered the big boss to say,

"You're right about her. I'll have two of my men eliminate the problem."

Neither Emily nor the Robo relaxed as they drove, but instead looked for anything that would trigger the contingency plan. When they spotted a suspicious car following, the Robo took action after he and Emily had belted in.

Accelerating onto a still-crowded surface street, he drove wildly, swerving into oncoming traffic, causing collisions, and dodging onto sidewalks, forcing pedestrians to leap out of the way, but the pursuer stayed with them. The Robo raced onto an elevated street, and when the pursuer did the same, he did a one-eighty and rammed into the pursuer, putting both cars out of commission. Then, he grabbed Emily as soon as both had climbed out and ran to the railing to gauge the distance and traffic below. The pursuers climbed out and staggered toward them with guns drawn, but before they could fire, the Robo leaped over with Emily clutched to his chest. When the pursuers reached the railing, the last thing they gaped at was Emily and the Robo escaping in the back of a pickup truck.

She celebrated their safe return to the hotel by ordering a slice of blueberry pie topped with two scoops of vanilla ice cream that she enjoyed with a Coke purchased from a vending machine. Then, she spliced and edited all the videos before making a backup copy that she put in an envelope along with a note nearly identical to what she had written for WGN. When finished, she called her A-Team contact.

"Pick us up at sunrise for the next leg of our trip."

"Ah, Miss Emily, we be there."

Emily told the driver to stop at the local station, KHOU-TV. When he did, she leaped out, gave the envelope to the security guard, and jumped back in before he could say a word.

When the airplane reached cruising altitude, Emily turned off the overhead light and her computer, then settled back to relax all the way to LA.

Chapter 10

September 2342

"Hunting in Los Angeles"

After arriving at the Hollywood Inn Suites, Emily divided her time between planning the tattler hunt and looking for Houston news story that would confirm that the Texas Matriarch senatorial candidate's opponent had been exposed. When it came several days later, she crossed Texas off her list and devoted all her energy to Los Angeles.

First, she constructed a list of top new-age-like places where she could attend crime victim meetings, including the Agape International Spiritual Center, Self-Realization Fellowship Hollywood Temple, and the Redondo Beach Center for Spiritual Living. Then, she researched the slum areas, so she could hold her own when talking with potential tattlers. She prepared one script for telling her story to a counselor and another for telling it to potential tattlers. Finally, she developed the plan to find tattlers. It would also make an incriminating video of a Matriarchate party candidate's main opponent.

Two days later, the Robo drove her mid-morning to the Agape Center that now occupied a Beverly Hills theater. Emily tried not to gawk like a tourist at the stylish buildings nearby, and when she entered, a greeter asked how she could help.

"Do you host meetings for crime victims?"

"What crimes are of interest?"

"Home burglary and financial looting."

"We do hold meetings, but I've never heard those crimes mentioned, but you're welcome to attend our meeting tonight."

"I'll try to make it."

Emily had similar results at the other locations on her list, but at least she had two more meetings to attend on succeeding days. She filled the time until this evening's meeting by having the Robo drive her through slum areas, making mental notes while he drove.

This is the safest-looking skid-row slum I've ever seen, and the people here look worthy of my sympathy, not danger or fear.

While attending, she looked and listened.

Everyone looks so stylish, and no one has problems like the ones I'm interested in. I can't spot a single tattler; I'll sneak out at the break.

When Emily had identical results at the other meetings, she had to revise her plan.

Maybe I'll spot something if I volunteer to work on the opponent's campaign. Tomorrow, I'll visit the campaign headquarters of Jacqueline Boyd.

Located in Boyd's congressional district, it occupied several storefronts in a strip mall that looked as ritzy as the district. When she walked in and announced she'd like to volunteer, one of the workers took her aside and said,

"What can you do?"

"I'm good with words, so I could write press releases or speeches."

"We're holding a meeting in a couple of minutes. Why don't you sit in and listen, and then follow me around for a day or two before making a commitment?"

"Thanks, that's a great idea…"

Doing so for the next day, Emily saw and heard nothing that would be the slightest bit useful, so she skipped out by mid-afternoon and told no one.

When she returned to the hotel, she searched online for information about Jacqueline Boyd. Three hours later, she summarized to herself.

That's one smart lady, still young and attractive. She pushes the issues that voters want, and her vibrant personality is one that the voters like. No wonder she's been elected multiple times. I think this is an example of a congresswoman who should be reelected.

I've struck out in LA, but two out of three is good, so I won't beat myself for coming up empty It's time to call the A-Team for a trip back to the Pequot Reservation.

When she announced this on the call, her regular contact said,

"Ah Miss Emily, we get you back to Pequot Reservation ASAP. We pick you up in couple hours, and I call when out front so you come meet us at entrance. Hokay?"

"Perfect. I'll be ready."

While waiting for the call, Emily thought of a final person to contact. Electra-C's avatar appeared, waiting for Emily to speak.

"I've had success in Chicago and Houston, but not in Los Angeles, and I'm out of ideas for LA. Do you have any suggestions?"

"Not even I can find relevant information if none exists online in Cyberspace, so it's time for you to move on."

"That's what I'll start doing on the flight home. I'll start prepping for a trip to Miami and New York City. Do you have any final thoughts?"

"Try not to place yourself in harm's way. Enlist my aid for another way."

Emily didn't have to say anything other than,

"OK, and bye for now," because the A-Team's call had just come in.

While riding to the airport, Emily knew what she would start doing on the flight. Four hours later, she had a plan, so she turned off the laptop and napped all the way home.

72

Chapter 11
October 2342

"A Most Dangerous Game"

Emily began planning her next two-city hunting trip to Miami and New York City. Focusing first on Miami, she followed essentially the same steps that had worked for Houston. She collected useful stats about the city, then built a list of new-age-like places that might hold crime-victim support group meetings where she might spot tattlers. And after that, she researched what areas drug smugglers worked. Finally, she assembled information about the opposing candidate. After three days of surfing, she printed what she had developed.

Hunting in Miami

- Miami's population of 500,000 ranks it the 42nd largest U.S. city.
- It's on the tip of Florida, making it a major entry point for South American drug trafficking, particularly from Colombia.
- I found three places that hold crime victim meetings: Unity on the Bay Spiritual Community (Palm Trees, in view of the ocean, immaculately maintained buildings, greenery, and shade trees), Vous Church, located in the Miami Gardens section (Situated in a converted church), and Miami Vineyard Community Church.
- Miami does have slums, particularly in Overtown. That's where the drug lords would work.
- I didn't find anything incriminating about our main opponent, Congressman Diego Lopez of the Guardian Party. If all else fails, I'll volunteer at his campaign headquarters to look for incriminating evidence.

Now that she had finished the plan, she called the A-Team to schedule the trip. When her normal contact answered, Emily gave all the details.

"Here's what I want for the two-city trip you'll set up. Fly me and my Robo from the Pequot Reservation to Miami's International Airport. Have a car waiting so we can drive to a downtown hotel, for which you'll make the reservation. I'll call when I've finished my work, and then you'll fly us to New York City's John F. Kennedy International Airport. I won't need hotel reservations or a car, and I know how to get back to the Pequot Reservation. Is that clear?"

"Ah yes, Miss Emily. Just tell when you want Pequot Reservation pickup."

"This coming Friday evening. That'll give me the weekend to prepare."

"Will do, Miss Emily. See you in two days."

Arriving early Saturday afternoon at the Port of Miami's Holiday Inn, Emily settled in before having a slice of lemon meringue pie and a Coke at the in-hotel restaurant. Afterwards, she walked around the nearby area, taking in all the surroundings.

The wide streets and sidewalks lined with palm trees seem so festive, as does the oceanfront marketplace on the other side of the wide and light-traffic boulevard. The hotels lining it aren't skyscrapers, but they are immaculate, and the view of Miami's oceanfront skyline of modern residential buildings is spectacular.

After reviewing her plan and story the next morning, she and the Robo drove through the slum area.

Gads, this slum is even cleaner than LA's, and the people look deserving of sympathy, not fear. But I do spot a group of guys wearing the same garb. They must be one of the city's notorious gangs.

Emily spent the rest of the day watching the news and binge-watching popular movies and TV series, going to bed early enough to be ready for action tomorrow morning.

Before entering the Vineland Community Church, she studied the building and others nearby.

What a pleasant-looking one-story beige-colored building with a red-tile roof. It blends in with the others. I hope it's as pleasant on the inside.

When she walked in and said she wanted to meet with a counselor, the greeter escorted Emily to the office of a pleasant-looking early-forties gentleman sitting behind a desk. He rose to shake her hand, then pointed to the chair across and spoke as soon as she sat.

"Good morning, señorita. How may I be of service?"

"I'm visiting important cities across the country, collecting information to write an article comparing crime victim meetings offered by New Age churches to traditional religions. Does your church hold them?"

"We do and give as much support as possible. And like most cities, we have many types of crimes. Are there any in particular you are investigating?"

"I would imagine Florida has many victims of drug trafficking."

Emily didn't need to say anything else. The fellow's cheerful expression became somber, like clouds covering the sun.

"No one has ever brought that up at any of the meetings I have hosted. It is a dangerous subject. In our city, drug pushers and the drug lords they report to are as powerful as the government. Those who testify against enter witness protection, and the news occasionally reports that one has just ended up dead."

"I didn't know. Thanks for telling me."

His cheerful expression returned when he said,

"But you are welcome to come to our meeting and see how it runs. We have one tomorrow evening at seven."

Emily said,

"Thanks for the invitation. I'll try to come," before leaving.

She had similar results at the other churches. Now she had three meetings on consecutive evenings, starting tomorrow.

Emily attended all three to get a better sense of Miami crime victims, but she came away with what she expected—not even a hint of a tattler. So, after the last meeting, she decided to look for a pusher the next evening.

Both the Robo and Emily dressed in shabby clothes and wore hidden microphones and cameras. And when they spotted at twilight a group of people who looked like they might be buying from a pusher, they parked far enough away to go unnoticed before shuffling into the crowd.

They blended in, but Emily made what could have been a fatal mistake. Her hidden camera came loose. The pusher's guards spotted what she was doing and fired a burst from semi-automatics. The Robo grabbed her, and they raced away.

Emily's frayed nerves kept her awake for hours. When she finally calmed down, she called the A-Team.

"I'm finished in Miami. We're ready to go to the Big Apple. We're driving right now to where you met us at the airport. Got that?"

"Ah, Miss Emily. I get. You might get there first. Hokay?"

"Sure thing. See you whenever."

By now, Emily considered New York City a second home, due to all the time she spent there, most recently at Senator Windstein's campaign headquarters. After arriving at a Midtown Manhattan hotel, she had room service bring her a hot fudge sundae, and when finished, started planning what she would do.

First, she reviewed the initial information about the New York Matriarch Party Candidate's main opponent, provided by Senator Windstein's campaign team.

Matriarchate Party Candidate: Angela Windstein

State: New York Position being Sought: Senator (Wants to be Re-Elected)

- Main Opponent Name: Hunter Bentley. Currently a three-term Congressman.
- Party: Democratic Party
- Close Campaign Associates: **CURRENTLY UNKNOWN**
- Crimes and Laws Opponent might be breaking: Prostitution
- Potential Tattlers: **CURRENTLY UNKNOWN**

Based on my hunting results, if the campaign team doesn't know the opponent's close campaign associates and potential tattlers, I'll strike out if I try to find them. And if Hunter Bentley is looking for prostitutes, he won't be out looking. He'll have them come to him. So, what can I do to his expose his lusty appetite for sex?

Emily started by surfing for information about Hunter, which she summarized an hour later.

He's a good-looking fellow with a personality people like. If I were looking for a sex partner, he'd be fun to play with. But what a hypocrite. He's always telling young people to avoid drugs and wait until they're in a committed relationship before having sex.

Emily relaxed for the next several hours, letting random thoughts stream into her brain. Suddenly, one of them snapped her to attention.

What did that sexy girl primping in the mirror say to me in the lounge at the speed dating club?...I got it...You're not a member, are you? I'd remember if you were. You'd be tough competition... That's it. I'll use my physical assets to expose Hunter. Tomorrow, I'll take the train and subway to Manhattan to purchase sexy attire for becoming a streetwalker, and to check out Bentley's campaign headquarters. I might want to become a volunteer.

Before going to bed, she made a list of what to buy: the sexiest black dress she could find and a bikini-thong. Then, she searched online for the Manhattan address of Bentley's campaign headquarters. She fell asleep pondering this problem.

Any prostitute he uses can't know his name, where he lives, or his political status. If they did, they could blackmail him. I'll bet he uses call girls…they're more discrete and don't display their profession to the public. This has possibilities.

By noon the next day, she had all the attire she needed after shopping at the Empire Exotics Lingerie and Clubwear and the Romantic Depot Sex Store. Then, she re-energized herself by ordering an enormous slice of New York cheesecake at the famous Barney Greengrass Deli and removing some calories by walking to the campaign headquarters. When she asked about volunteering, one worker replied with a question she knew would be coming.

"What skills do you have that we could use?"

"I'm good with words. I could write press releases and help with speeches."

"That might work, but Hunter's very particular. He'll have to meet you."

"Does he drive here often?"

"Several times a week, and like the rest of us, he parks in the street lot down the block. You can't miss his car. It has the vanity plate NYC TOP PICK. He'll be here tomorrow morning, so come back then. We get here by eight to beat the traffic."

"Thanks. I'll try to be here."

By the time she reached home, she knew what she and the Robo would do tomorrow.

The Robo drove to Manhattan early enough the next morning to park in the street lot down the block, and when she spotted the vanity plate, she told the Robo to plant a tracker on the car. After that, she and the Robo poked around in the Metropolitan Museum of Art, American Museum of Natural History, and the Museum of Illusions, and when the tracker showed Hunter's car was on the move, they rushed back so the Robo could follow him.

Now I'll know where he lives and parks his car. I'll be able to track him when he's on the move.

But Emily was not yet ready to play the streetwalker or call girl role. Early the next morning, she and the Robo drove back to Hunter's home in a typical middle-class neighborhood, parking in an out-of-the-way location where they could see when he drove away. When he did, Emily placed a call to Electra-C.

"My Robo and I want to break into Hunter Bentley's house and garage. If I give you his address, can you disable all alarms?'

"I will do that immediately. Call me when you are ready to leave."

"Will do. And could you look for patterns in his comings and goings from the house? Maybe you can find a time when he's always someplace else, so I can accidentally run into him on purpose."

Electra-C's reply matched Emily's.

"Will do."

The Robo had all the tools needed to pick the locks. After placing a tracker on Hunter's other car, they entered the house, looking for any hidden cameras he might use to film himself and a call girl in action, and they found a fully equipped basement bedroom. The Robo spotted a hidden camera, and that sparked a thought.

I could place my own hidden camera, but then someone would have to monitor it 24-7, and if he found it, I'd be SOL. Besides, it might take too long to catch him in the act, and I have to get the evidence ASAP, so a camera is a no-go.

Emily had one last task to complete before taking on the role of streetwalker. She had to find a couple of prostitutes who would be willing to join in a most dangerous game. She waited until Saturday evening to start.

The Robo dropped her off at a Manhattan location known for its prostitution and john activity. She used her insouciantly sexy saunter to attract attention, turning down offers from the guys driving by, but when a prostitute approached, she launched into her story.

"How would you and one of your friends like to dump your johns?"

Those words grabbed attention.

"How so?"

"You can go into business with me. Your johns will never catch on."

"What do we have to do?"

"Just drive around with me, and we'll find guys that want to do business with us."

"I know someone who'd be interested, my roommate, but the three of us had better meet."

"That's the plan. How about tonight?"

"It's been slow, so why not?"

"OK, come with me to my car; then, we'll pick up your friend."

Emily followed the tracker signals back to the Robo's car. Before climbing in, the prostitute checked out the car.

"Jesus, what is that. Is it human?"

"That's our protection in case a customer wants more than he should get."

Two hours later, the three ladies were sitting at a booth in an all-night diner. Emily started the conversation.

"Call me Elfie; that's my street name. What are yours?"

The brunette said,

"Mine's Trixie, and my roommate goes by Ezee. Guys always expect blondes to be easy."

"Please give me your address and phone number, so I can pick you up when we're ready to prowl."

After doing so, Trixie asked a reasonable question.

"When do you think that'll be?"

"Soon, I hope. And whenever we're on the prowl, have a lady's gym bag packed with what you need. Do you have a car?"

"No, but why would we need one if you'll be driving?"

"There'll be times you need to drive, and Mr. Protection will be tailing us. Don't worry, I'll tell you in advance. Anything else you want to ask?"

Trixie and Ezee looked at one another before Trixie said,

"No".

"Well, I'll drive you home."

Emily had difficulty containing her excitement, but controlled herself for two days before calling Electra-C.

Electra-C knew from Emily's animated greeting the reason she was calling, but she waited patiently for her to explain.

"I want to bump into Hunter. Have you figured out where and when?"

"Your Mr. Bentley drives every weekday at six p.m. to a nearby strip mall, and according to the surveillance cameras I hacked into, he has something to eat at the Lucky Grill."

"Perfect, I'll do it tomorrow. Thanks."

Electra-C merely smiled before her avatar vanished.

Then she called her newest partners. Recognizing Trixie's voice, Emily said,

"I'll pick you and Ezee up tomorrow at 4 p.m. We won't need protection, so one car will do it. Dress in a sexy outfit and pack a lady's bag just in case our potential client wants action, but tomorrow's simply a meet and greet. Wear something sexy, and when we get there, follow me into the strip mall's diner and act naturally. Let me do all the talking, OK?"

Emily detected humor in Trixie's voice when she said,

"Oh, I get it. You can introduce him to the lay of the land."

Emily laughed before saying,

"That's the plan. Get ready to start playing the game."

Emily recognized Hunter's car when she parked in the strip mall's lot, then her partners followed close behind as she began her act. She sauntered toward his booth but accidentally bumped into it, causing the water in his glass to cascade onto his lap.

"Oh, dear me, I'm so sorry."

Hunter responded with a generous smile while saying,

"No harm done. Lots worse has happened."

Emily let her coquettish smile answer, and then she walked to a booth where she could watch him. When her partners sat on the opposite side, she said,

"Just pretend we're talking about the weather. I'll let you know when the guy walks toward us."

Sure enough, two minutes later, Hunter motioned to his waitress and pointed toward Emily before prancing to her table.

"May I join you?"

Emily changed into Elfie and wore her coquettish expression before saying,

"Please do, and I promise not to spill anything else."

When Hunter's pleasing manners and table-talk charmed her partners, Elfie played along. After the waitress brought their dinners, Hunter eventually asked what Elfie knew he would.

"Do you ladies normally dress so pleasingly when going out?"

Elfie sighed, then said,

"It's part of the job."

She and Hunter chatted for ten more minutes before he said,

"My name's Hunter, what's yours?"

"I'm Elfie." She nodded to her partners, who answered,

"I'm Trixie," followed by,

"I'm Ezee."

Hunter's words bubbled when he said,

"Why don't you give me a phone number so we can get together again. I'm usually busy weekdays, but I always reserve Saturday night for fun."

After Trixie gave her number, Elfie rose before saying,

We have to go to work now. Call us sometime."

Elfie's partners followed her, with Hunter right behind. When they reached her car, he said,

"Why don't we meet back here this coming Saturday evening at eight?"

"Elfie looked at Trixie, who gave a thumbs up for herself and Ezee, before saying,

"That sounds good. We'll be ready to have a good time, and you should too. We'll be back."

On the drive back to her partners' place, Emily issued commands.

"You have all of tomorrow to rent a car and pack your lady's bags. And for Saturday night, get ready to wear your sexiest dress on the outside that covers your sexiest bikini thong on the inside. Mr. Protection will drive me to your place so we get there by 6:30 p.m. Then you'll drive the three of us to the Lucky Grill so we get there a little after 8:00. Mr. Protection will tail us, and I'll tell you more as we drive to meet Hunter. Any questions?"

There were none.

Emily packed her bag on Friday morning with everything needed, including her pistol and a can of Mace, just in case an emergency came up before the Robo could rescue them. She rigged her bag with a hidden camera and microphone so she could record Hunter in action before laying out what she would wear.

After that, she alternated between practicing her story and rehearsing what she would do, and when she became too wound up, she went for a run to unwind. All that took her to early evening, when she binge-watched for relaxation.

Emily kept as calm as possible until leaving the next day by remembering a quote from a famous athlete.

Don't leave your gold-medal performance in the gym… I won't wear myself out by rehearsing too much for tonight.

Looking nervous, Trixie and Ezee were waiting in the rental car when the Robo pulled up. Erin jumped into the back seat, and Trixie drove with the Robo tailing far enough behind to become nearly unnoticeable.

Emily felt her racing pulse and trembling hands stop.

It feels so good to have the waiting over. I prefer action to anticipation.

Then, her reassuring words started flowing.

"Your streetwalking experience has already exposed you to anything Hunter might ask for, so once the clothes start coming off, just act naturally because you know what to do. And until the action begins, let me do all the talking and negotiating, OK?"

The tone of Emily's voice had loosened Trixie enough to ask a question.

"Do you think Hunter will drive us to his place?"

"Yes, and he'll drive us back to yours when he's had enough."

That prompted Ezee to ask,

"What do you think his place will be like?"

"I think it'll have a bedroom all set up for sex, but it'll be the same as what you've seen before, so just act naturally. And act bored, not excited. We're doing Hunter a big favor."

By the time they parked next to Hunter, all the ladies pretended to look bored. Hunter spoke as soon as they stood in front of his car, holding their gym bags.

"How lovely you look. Hop in and I'll drive to where the action is about to begin," but Emily had other ideas.

"Let's set the rules. How much will you pay each of us?"

"Five hundred dollars apiece should be more than enough."

"For how long?"

"Judging from the way you look and how I feel, I should be good until midnight."

Elfie looked at her partners, who agreed.

Hunter led them to the basement bedroom and waited outside for the girls to get ready. Emily made sure she clustered the bags at a spot where her hidden camera and microphone would capture all the action on the bed. Then, after removing their high-heeled shoes and dresses, and calling for Hunter to enter, the action began.

The ladies worked as a team, playfully undressing him. His laughter and flushed cheeks revealed his growing excitement, and he became even more animated when he started removing their string bikinis. By the time everyone was down to the bare essentials, he looked ready for more.

He grabbed Elfie and said,

"You're first," before placing her face up on the bed. Trixie and Ezee backed away, but before he could take the next step, Elfie sprang her surprise.

"I don't think you should go all the way with me tonight. When I tested this morning, I came up positive for the latest STD infection."

Hunter pulled back but didn't slow down. He booted Elfie off bed and, after throwing Ezee on, picked up where he had left off.

The action continued until Hunter's stamina wore out. When he collapsed, all the ladies in the chairs grouped in a corner, waiting for him to say something.

He eventually sat up and said,

"Tonight ranks among the top three nights ever."

Elfie said,

"You hung in there, fine and dandy. Now, it's time for all of us to get dressed, so you can pay me before driving us back to our car."

Hunter let them shower and then gave them a Coke before doing so an hour later.

All the ladies relaxed on the drive home, waiting for Emily to speak.

"Great work from the two of you. That's why I'm giving each of you seven hundred dollars."

Trixie said,

"You did a great job handling all the details, but it seems like you deliberately picked Hunter. Why's that?"

"Whether I did or didn't, you don't need to know. Just be happy with the payoff, OK?"

"OK."

No one spoke again until the Robo was ready to drive away. That's when Ezee asked,

"When do you think we'll do this again?"

"I'll let you know in a couple of days. Stay healthy and safe until then."

Emily decompressed on the drive home but had more to do before trying to sleep. She edited the video to make sure it captured everything needed to show Hunter's lust for sex. Then, she made a backup copy, putting it in an addressed envelope along with a note similar to the one she had used for KHOU-TV. Then, she addressed it to any investigative reporter at the local station, WABC-TV.

When finished, she glanced at her cell phone.

It's almost 5 a.m., but I can't fall asleep until I deliver the goods. My Robo can drive me to the station's studio. It's open 24-7.

Climbing out of the back seat, Emily trudged to the guard at the entrance and gave him the envelope, but she said nothing. Then, she trudged back and climbed in. She could now sleep all the way home.

Chapter 12
November 2342

"Warnings from Electra-C"

Emily needed two full days to re-energize after returning from playing her most dangerous game. And she called Trixie early that morning. When she answered on the third ring, Emily started talking.

"How are you and Ezee after we played around with Hunter? The action wore me out, and I needed to rest for the next two days."

Trixie's laugh preceded her words.

"We're fine. After all, we did nothing but act naturally, but you handled all the stressful stuff. How long until you arrange our next outing?"

"Not until I get rid of the latest STD infection. How about I call you in a week to let you know what progress I'm making?"

"That'll work. Call me then."

"Will do; bye for now."

With that call out of the way, Emily contacted Electra-C, whose avatar appeared on the screen immediately and listened patiently until Emily finished fifteen minutes later. The tone of Electra-C's words matched the avatar's concerned expression.

"I'm pleased you enjoy being a crime stopper, but you're taking too many chances that put you in harm's way. As you move into your future, I will instruct Lily on planning and implementing the things you choose to do, and I will create your new business, similar to Twilight World Consulting Services, which I'll name

Crime Stoppers Anonymous, or CSA for short. And I'll do for it the same as I'm doing for TW—you tell me what you want to research, and I'll generate the report."

"I like this; what do you think I should start with?"

"You're clever with words, so that's for you to decide. If you choose something that fits with your TW client projects, they might become CSA clients as well."

"Now I know what to do. I'll start thinking about it and talk with Lily once I've picked it. And I assume Lily will keep you posted."

"That's the plan. Take care."

Electra-C's avatar vanished.

After taking the next two days to choose her first topic for launching CSA Consulting, Emily explained it to Lily at breakfast after running.

"I'm going to research the impact on the geopolitical order caused by the European Union replacing the U.S.-Russian Alliance as the second superpower, leaving China on top, followed by the EU, then the Indian-African Alliance, and the U.S-Russian Alliance a distant fourth. The American people want the U.S. government to dump Russia and chart a path back to greatness, but it's by no means certain."

"That's an excellent choice. Some of your current TW clients will want to get your CSA reports, so contact them soon. And while you're doing that, you should read the Bible and interpret it not as a collection of children's Sunday School stories but as a compilation of the greatest controversies in early Christian history."

"I've heard about some that come from the Dead Sea Scrolls. It reported rumors about Jesus and Mary Magdalene becoming husband and wife, and spending the rest of their lives traveling and living among the twelve tribes of Israel."

"Good, that gives you a head start in your Bible studies, which will sharpen your analytic skills and teach what the future might hold, at least from what the Bible predicts. You'll find that the future might be a dangerous place, neither kinder nor gentler."

Emily rubbed the back of her neck before saying,

"I'll have plenty to do in preparation for America's declining superpower status, but the saying that 'forewarned is forearmed' applies, and with you, Electra-C, and Indira to rely on, any crime stopper assignments I take should be manageable."

Lily's tone added a final note of caution.

"All of us hope so."

Chapter 13
December 2342

"Hunting for CSA Clients"

After taking the morning to prepare the best prospect's target list for CSA Consulting, Emily took a moment to review what she had developed.

Best Prospects for CSA Consulting Clients

Prospect	Source	Reasons Why
Angela Windstein & Matriarch Party	From my Campaign Work	Americans want a better government that will restore the Country's Superpower status, which my Reports Highlight
Pew Research Organization	Angela Windstein	Should like my Reports that point to potential Socio-Pol. Agitators.
European Headquarters in DC	Angela Windstein	Needs to strengthen both Defensive and Offensive Capability, now that U.S might not assist. My reports provide Assessment
NOAA	Univ. Chgo Climate Change Institute	Growing World Awareness that Climate Change is a Shared Responsibility
Indian-African Alliance	Electra-C	The Alliance via Zimbabwean and Monet Banda needs to know the impact of the U.S. no longer being among the superpowers.

All of them are in DC, which should make travel efficient. I might be able to meet with several during the same trip.

Emily spent the next three days arranging trips to meet with all during a series of three separate trips. On each, she would have the A-Team pick up Lily, one Robo, and herself at the Pequot Reservation, and have a car waiting in DC. She would make hotel reservations if needed.

A week later, the Robo was driving to their first meeting. It would be held mid-morning at Senator Windstein's office in the Senate Office Building. After the Robo dropped them off, Lily surprised Emily by telling her about the building complex.

"The three U.S. Senate buildings are the Russell, Dirksen, and Hart. Underground tunnels connect them. The Russell is the oldest and an example of Beaux-Arts architecture. It was the first of the three to be constructed. Would you like to hear more?"

"Sure, but what's Beau-Arts architecture?"

"It's a theatrical and highly ornamented classical style that emerged in Paris during the 19th century. It combines Greek and Roman design principles with Renaissance and Baroque influences, characterized by order, symmetry, grandiosity, and elaborate detail, which was popular for public buildings like train stations, museums, and government buildings from the late 19th to early 20th centuries, but is no longer in use. The second is the Dirksen Building, named after Illinois Senator Everett Dirksen, whose most famous quote goes like this—A billion here and a billion there and pretty soon you're talking real money. And the third is the Hart Building, named after Senator Philip Hart. It's the most modern. He represented Colorado in the Senate from 1975 to 1987, and was the front-runner for the 1984 and 1988 Democratic presidential nominations, but dropped out of the latter campaign amid revelations of extramarital affairs."

Emily made a final comment before they entered Senator Windstein's office.

"That's good to know. It shows what happens when the press reports that a politician has violated the public's morality. I'll file that away in case I ever decide to run for office. Now remember, let me do all the talking."

Lily nodded.

Emily started talking as soon as they were sitting in the chairs the Senator had just pointed to.

"I think this is the first time you're meeting Lily Lloyd, my office administrator and personal assistant. We're pleased you won re-election and are here to recommend you subscribe to CSA Consulting—our new service company."

"I might if I knew what CSA stands for."

"Crime Stoppers Anonymous. It digs up information on people or organizations that might cause problems for the reasons clients specify. You saw how well it worked on your main opponent."

"I can't imagine how it uncovered his healthy appetite for sex, but it did the trick. I'll subscribe."

"Thank you, and I'll come back in early January to discuss what you would like me to investigate."

"Is there anything else you'd like to talk about?"

"Lily would like a tour of the underground tunnel network. Is there one starting soon?"

"How about now? Please be my guest. After all, I'm here in large part thanks to you."

Later that day, they met with their contact at the European Union office, speaking as soon as they were sitting on a sofa.

I've launched a new consulting business, CSA, that's a sister to TW Consulting. CSA stands for Crime Stoppers Anonymous, and

I think you should subscribe. Your customized reports might give you insights and forecasts regarding building your offensive and defensive capabilities now that the U.S. has dropped out of NATO."

"How do I subscribe?"

"Just like you're doing for TW Consulting. I'll send you weekly reports and contact you to discuss them further."

"Sign me up."

The second trip started a week later, following the same procedure. This time, she met first with her contact at the PEW Organization and achieved similar results after explaining CSA. After that, she met with her NOAA contact, who, seeing the value its reports would provide, subscribed immediately.

That left one more trip. A week later, she and Lily were sitting in Monet's office in the Zimbabwean Embassy. After Monet's diplomatically cordial greeting, Emily said,

"I don't remember if I ever introduced Lily, my office manager and personal assistant."

"I don't believe so. How did you find her?"

After summarizing, Emily proceeded to the main reason for her visit.

"I've just launched a new consulting business, CSA, which stands for Crime Stoppers Anonymous. You can subscribe just like you're subscribing to TW Consulting, and I'll send you weekly customized reports that will analyze the impact on the Indian-African Alliance caused by the U.S. no longer being a superpower."

Monet's calm voice gave the answer Emily wanted.

"I'll subscribe."

Now that Emily had everything taken care of just before the start of the holiday season, she knew what to do next, and she explained it to Lily.

"It's time to relax while planning some projects for next year and doing some binge-watching. How do you like that?"

"I'm designed to need no relaxation, but I'll keep you company."

"Good. I always enjoy your company."

Chapter 14
January 2343

"Armageddon Unleashed"

Emily sang a popular children's song streaming through her memory as she completed her first run of the New Year.

The Sun comes up in the early morn, over the meadows of morning. Banners of day in the East are hung, the early lark has sung…

When finally finished with both the run and song, she took several deep breaths before saying more to herself.

Here we are, Friday, January 1st, and I've already started my New Year's resolution to get in better shape…and after breakfast, I'll have a weight set, a sit-up bench, and a chinning bar delivered to the Pequot Deus Lab so Lily and I can set up a fitness center.

After explaining to Lily what they would soon be doing, Emily said,

"This afternoon, one of our Robos will drive us to the Broadway play 'The Sound of Music.' That should be a delightful way to start the New Year."

"Yes, and although your emotional persona is better, mine will enjoy it too…"

By the time they left for the 6 p.m. performance, the weather had changed, as the storm predicted for tomorrow began rolling in earlier, but Lily said that would be no problem because the Robo would drop them off in front of the theater. However, as they were nearing it, Emily's cell phone chimed, and when she answered on the second ring, she recognized Electra-C's voice, whose tone matched the alarming message.

"A submarine has just surfaced in the Port of New York to launch a barrage of atomic-tipped ICBMs. You have ten minutes to contact your closest friends before seeking shelter in

the deepest subway station."

When Emily's brain froze, Lily shook her until she snapped out of the stupor.

"Jesus, stop the car. Who did it? What should I do after making the calls?"

Electra-C said,

"A Chinese submarine. Now, warn others and contact me when it's safe to come out." Then, her voice vanished.

Emily hastily rehearsed a message she would repeat to her closest DC friends.

Don't talk, just listen. A Chinese submarine has just launched atomic ICBMs. One will hit DC in less than 30 minutes, so seek a safe place underground. I'm doing the same in NYC. Good luck to all of us. I hope we survive this Armageddon that's just been unleashed.

After speaking or leaving messages, she led the mad dash to the nearest subway station. There was no panic in the streets because the launch had not yet been detected, so Lily, the Robo, and Emily were the first to reach the lowest platform and find a place to sit. When her panic subsided, Emily said,

"Stay here while I get some candy bars and cans of Coke."

When she returned fifteen minutes later, people had begun streaming in, so Emily and her companions said nothing.

Suddenly, a distant blast sent a shock wave through the platform, buckling the floor and plunging everything into blackness. People started screaming, but Emily and her crew didn't. An eerie calm came over her, and it triggered words that echoed in her head.

If we survive, what will I do when it's safe to climb out? Right now, I haven't a clue, but when we get to the surface, I'll contact Electra-C. If enough of the Twilight World survives, she'll know what to do.

THE END